"Love looks not with the eyes, but with the mind,
And therefore is wing'd Cupid painted blind."

So Shakespeare said.
His words will still ring true
As long as roses blush their famous red
And violets, blue.

Contents

Prologue

In a laboratory outpost on a sweep of icy wasteland in Antarctica, a man with a black beard reread the note he'd just written. He chewed the edges of his mustache, then folded the message into an envelope. He scribbled the address with an impatient hand: *Tyburn Road, Hamlet, Vermont.* Since he was on a research mission for the U.S. government, he only needed a regular stamp, though the letter would travel thousands of miles before reaching its destination. He looked at the stamps he had. In brightly colored block letters, one of them said LOVE.

He sighed, and chose a stamp with a picture of a penguin on it instead.

The scientist had a sister who lived in Greece. That very same day, she hauled a big box to the main post office in Athens. She opened her purse, spilling drachmas toward the man behind the counter. In Greek, she chattered at him. "Overseas mail. For my niece in America. Hurry, it's a present for her."

"How do you want to send it?" asked the man patiently, reaching for a customs declaration form.

"With love," said the woman, and kissed the name on the box, to prove it. "Valentine's Day is coming, and I want her to remember how much I love her. She's having a hard year. Send it the quickest way you can. Airmail special delivery. Express, deluxe, VIP service: whichever is fastest."

The Greek postal clerk didn't know, of course, that the box from Athens was heading to the same place as the letter from Antarctica: a house on Tyburn Road, Hamlet, Vermont, USA. He didn't know that sometimes winter in Vermont can feel as cold as Antarctica. He knew only that you had to be careful in the handling of precious messages. He stamped FRAGILE all over the box—but he stamped it gingerly, in case there was something breakable inside.

Which there was.

1

My Bloody Valentine

I hate you!"

"I hate you double!"

Thekla Mustard and Sammy Grubb stared at each other. Everyone else in the classroom fell silent, watching the test of wits.

"I hate you to the ten-billionth power," said Thekla.

"I hate you to the ten-billionth-plus-one power," Sammy answered.

"I hate you until the end of time," she said.

"I hate you until the end of time and a week later," he replied.

"I hate you to the farthest depths of space."

"I hate you to the farthest depths of space and a mile farther."

"I hate you"—Thekla Mustard paused for inspiration—"I hate you more than I hate homework."

"Wow." Sammy Grubb was impressed. He couldn't beat that. "You must really hate me a lot. But may I borrow your red crayon anyway? Mine is all used up."

"Sure, why not?" said Thekla, and handed it over.

Miss Earth, the teacher, said, "Thekla and Sammy. Such loud scorn for each other! Sometimes people who

1

show dislike so publicly are really trying to hide their affection. Did you ever think of that?"

Sammy Grubb and Thekla Mustard clamped their mouths shut. Not another word! How awful if anyone imagined that the famous rivals actually liked each other. Both of them would prefer to suffer an instant painful death than to be thought—shudder—*in love*.

"Now, children," said Miss Earth. "Today is Wednesday. Saint Valentine's Day is on Friday. We're going to make Valentine's Day cards."

The sun slid behind a cloud. The room went chilly. The snow seemed to grip the windowsills with frozen white mittens. The hearts of about a dozen kids sank at exactly the same instant. Valentine's Day. What if nobody sends me a card? What if somebody *does* send me a card? What'll I do *then*? A certain variety of panic clutched many sets of guts. Valentine's Day was supposed to be a holiday, but sometimes it seemed like a nightmare. Love was scarier than spiders, ghosts, and aliens put together.

Miss Earth, generally alert to the mood of the classroom, today seemed a bit out to lunch. She blathered on. "I want to make sure that everyone gets a valentine and nobody is left out, so we're going to have a drawing. People, write your name on a sheet of paper and crumple it up. Put it in this bag. That's it. Everybody? Good."

"We had Valentine's Day in India," said Salim, who was the new student this year. "What's the holiday like in the United States, I wonder?"

"Who wants to tell Salim about Valentine's Day?" said Miss Earth.

The boys sat on their hands. All the girls except Pearl waved their arms around hysterically. "Fawn Petros," said Miss Earth. "You say what you know."

"Valentine's Day is when cupids fly through the air and they, like, have these arrows," said Fawn. "Like poisoned darts or something. They hit you and—*kapow*—it's love at first sight."

"Sounds pretty stupid to me," said Salim.

"Don't say stupid," said Miss Earth. "That's rude. Say *puzzling*."

Fawn continued. "You can't control yourself. You, like, start kissing frogs and stuff."

Salim looked doubtfully at the frog in the terrarium. The frog was named Kermit in honor of the famous Muppet. The students called him Kermit the Hermit. He was a nervous sort and liked to be left alone. He went and hid behind his rock. "Kissing frogs?" said Salim. "I hope not."

"Fawn is telling you part of a legend," said Miss Earth. "The ancient Greeks honored a spirit they called Eros, who was usually pictured as a handsome young man with wings. He could make people fall in love with each other. The ancient Romans called the same figure Cupid; eventually, cupids came to be pictured as small winged children who liked to cause romantic mischief. But that's all storytelling. Historically, Saint Valentine was an early martyr of the Christian church. His life had no connection with the kind of greeting cards we send. Long ago, people believed that birds first began to mate on the day that was later chosen for Saint Valentine's feast day. So now we have come to think of Valentine's Day as a time for sweethearts of all sorts. Nice that it comes in cold February, isn't it? Our hearts are warmed by this simple custom. We show our friends that we love them by sending cards. Okay, end of commercial.

"Now, class, each of you will draw a name from this paper bag. If you pick your own name, please put it back. Then you can make Valentine's Day cards while I read aloud."

One by one the tense hearts relaxed. This was affection by lottery, so nobody could lose. One by one the students came forward and pulled scraps of paper out of Miss Earth's paper sack. "What if a boy gets a boy's name?" said Stan Tomaski.

"Valentine's Day is for friends as well as sweethearts," said Miss Earth firmly.

"What if a secret admirer wants to send a card to me?" said Thekla Mustard, tossing her curly hair prettily. The entire class said, *"Oooooooooooh."*

Miss Earth said, "Secret admirers keep their affection secret. That's the whole idea. They'll have to do it on their own time, Thekla. Now, my little sweethearts, get to work. Remember, be kind."

The class drew and painted hearts while their teacher sat in the reading rocker and began to read a story from the book of fairy tales. The girls drew perfect red hearts, surrounded by cupids doing target practice. The boys drew lots of hearts, too—hearts stabbed with knives, hearts ripped from chests, hearts still beating, dripping blood. The red crayon was very popular.

Sammy Grubb groaned. The slip of paper he had pulled from the sack said *Thekla Mustard*. Thekla Mustard was the Empress of the Tattletales, a club made up of girls in the class. "Be mine, Frankenstein," he wrote. Then he improved on it. By the time he was done he had a whole little poem. It went like this:

> Be mine, Frankenstein.
> Be my bloody valentine!
> Won't you come along and dine?
> Have some rotten porcupine.
> Have a slurp of turpentine.
> If your stomach gets abysmal
> And you're feeling kinda dismal
> Have some poisoned Pepto-Bismol.

By a twist of fate, Thekla Mustard had selected Sammy Grubb's name. He was the Chief of the Copycats, the boys' club. Thekla didn't feel lovey-dovey toward Sammy Grubb. In fact, sometimes she couldn't stand him. But Thekla knew a little bit of poetry by John Keats. And wasn't Keats known to be a *Romantic* poet? So she managed to work an annoying quotation from Keats into her card. It said:

> Beauty is truth, truth beauty,
> So won't you be my sweet patootie?

That should shut Sammy Grubb up good and proper!

Pearl Hotchkiss picked Fawn Petros's name. Pearl was the only kid in the class who didn't belong to either of the clubs. She called herself a free thinker. Thinking freely, she didn't mind making a valentine for Fawn. Pearl worked hard on her valentine. All bows and ribbons and plump hearts. She was proud of it, but she wished she could give it to Sammy Grubb instead. Once in a while Pearl liked Sammy, but not *romantically*—and, besides, she didn't want anyone to know about it. Maybe she should do a *secret admirer* card for him. Hmm.

Fawn Petros was more of a slow thinker than a free one. She liked holidays. She sounded out the letters of the name she had pulled. *Salim Bannerjee.* She would work on a card for him soon. But first she wanted to finish the one she'd already started. It was ornate and beautiful. It was for someone very important. Someone not in the class. She wasn't sure she would send it. She would wait and see.

"Isn't that a beautiful fairy tale?" said Miss Earth when she had finished.

All the girls except Pearl thought it was wonderfully romantic. Pearl thought it was dumb.

"I loved it when the heroine died," said Thekla. "So moving!"

"Somebody dies?" said Sammy. "I forgot to listen. I hope it was gruesome."

"She died of love," said Thekla.

"Oh, please," said Sammy. "I'm glad I wasn't listening. I'd have died of boredom."

Miss Earth touched the corner of her eye with a cloth handkerchief sporting her initials—*M.E.,* for Miss Earth. She cleared her throat and said, "The poor little milkmaid did die of love. A kind of heart attack, I guess. Not a bad story, even if Valentine's Day isn't one of my favorite holidays of the year."

She paused, and stammered, and dropped the reading book to the floor. She couldn't go on. Was the memory of love having its way with her? The kids watched with alarm. "Glass of water, Miss Earth?" said Moshe Cohn. "Hey, somebody, catch her! She's going to faint!"

The Ugly Vase

A few moments later Miss Earth blinked and stammered, "Wh—wh—where am I?"

"Germaine Earth," said Nurse Pinky Crisp crisply, "you are lying flat out on a braided rug. Right in your own classroom in the Josiah Fawcett Elementary School in Hamlet, Vermont. Lawsy, where did you think you were? Timbuktu?"

Miss Earth said, "Help me up."

"Nothing doing," said Nurse Crisp. "Not till I take your blood pressure. You had a bad tumble there. If your students hadn't broken your fall, you'd have gotten a nasty wallop on the noggin. Good work, kids. Thanks for coming to get me."

They shrugged. All in the line of duty.

Nurse Crisp took Miss Earth's pulse, felt her forehead, and examined her fingernails for unsightly breakage. "You're right as rain," announced the school nurse. "But what made you check out for a moment?"

"A sad memory," said Miss Earth. "It won't happen again."

"Ah, memories," said Nurse Crisp mysteriously. "Sooner or later they're all sad, aren't they?"

"I don't know," said Miss Earth. "I'm too young to be certain of that. I sure hope not."

"Well, live and learn," said Nurse Crisp. "Now, I must get back to the kindergartners and check their ears for waxy buildup."

Shakily, Miss Earth sat down at her desk. She groped through her lunch bag for something to give her strength. She found a jelly doughnut. When she bit into it, the jelly plopped out onto her open attendance book.

"Look!" said Fawn Petros. "Miss Earth's jelly fell in the shape of a heart!"

It was true. Miss Earth looked pale again.

"Miss Earth," said Thekla Mustard sternly. "What is the *matter* with you today?"

"Oh, all right. I confess," said Miss Earth. "Thoughts of Valentine's Day always make me think of the man I was once going to marry. I told you about him. The one who got run over by the Santa Claus float at the Macy's Thanksgiving Day Parade. You see, I loved him dearly."

"Did you call him your valentine?" said Sammy Grubb.

"Did you call him your sweet patootie?" said Thekla Mustard.

"Did you send him cards signed 'from a secret admirer'?" asked Fawn Petros.

"What was his name?" said Pearl Hotchkiss.

"That's private," said Miss Earth. "Please. I miss him, you see. Every now and then I remember how much it hurts. My heart is still broken." Then she cleared her throat and began to look at her book of lesson plans as if she meant business.

Fawn Petros scooted forward and scooped up the book of fairy tales from the floor. She thought: I know what it's like to miss someone that much.

At the Hamlet House of Beauty, Gladys Petros held the hand mirror. Her customer, Widow Wendell, oohed and aahed. The Widow Wendell's head was a dome of curls. It looked like a shell of silver-blue caramelized seaweed. "Glorious," said Widow Wendell. "I feel like a million bucks."

"Well, you don't owe me a million bucks. You owe me twelve fifty," said Mrs. Petros.

Fawn came clomping into the shop, shivering from the cold. "Mom, Miss Earth fainted today, all because of a broken heart," she said.

Widow Wendell and Mrs. Petros exchanged glances in the mirror. "The poor dear," said Widow Wendell. "If only she could get over him—"

"Who?" said Fawn. "She's never told us his name."

"Then it's not my business to inform you," said Widow Wendell with a smug manner. She paid for her beauty treatment and put on her overcoat and boots, and went sailing out into the cutting February wind, a picture of Yankee loveliness, age seventy-two and holding the fort nicely, if she did say so herself.

Fawn straightened the magazines on the rack. "Why won't Miss Earth tell us the name of her dead sweetheart?"

"Ours is not to reason why, ours is but to wash and dry," said Mrs. Petros, brushing silver-blue strands off the seat of the hair-drying chair. "Oh, by the way, there's a package for you. From your Aunt Sophia in Greece."

"Neat," said Fawn. She loved her Aunt Sophia. In her aunt's ratchety writing, Fawn read:

Dear Fawn,

Here's a Valentine's Day gift for my favorite niece! I found it in the Plaka, the market-place just below the Acropolis. I don't think it's very old or valuable, or I wouldn't send it by mail. So if it arrives to you in pieces, just think of it as a Valentine's puzzle! But I hope you like it. Kiss your mom for me, and lotsa hugs for the holiday.

Your loving Aunt Sophia

This was followed by a row of hearts and *X*'s and *0*'s, like this:

♡ X O ♡ X O ♡ X O ♡ X O ♡ X O ♡ X O

Fawn got a pair of scissors that her mom used for hair-cutting. She snipped the string of the parcel and tore open the brown paper. The box was stuffed with crumpled-up Greek newspapers. Fawn let them fall on the floor until she had her hands on something solid.

"I don't think it's broken," she said, and pulled it out of the box.

It was a sort of vase or jug. Painted brick red, with white lines scratched in the surface. On either side, two handles flared out.

"Ooh, that's some ugly piece of junk," said Gladys Petros, who preferred presents with fringe if possible. "What's drawn on it? Babies being catapulted by circus cannons?"

"No, look, the babies have bows and arrows," said Fawn. "Cupids. The little true-love guys. We were talking about them in school."

"Oh," said her mother. "True love. Isn't that nice." (Mrs. Petros didn't think much of true love anymore. Ever since her scientist husband was stationed in Antarctica, he came home only once a year.)

The vase had a clay stopper stuck in the narrow neck. Wax was dribbled all over it, as if someone had wanted to make sure that the stopper wouldn't come out. Fawn shook the vase. It sounded hollow. Or was there a faint rustle inside? Dried bugs? Or something else?

"We could wire that vase and buy a pretty fringed lampshade for it," said her mother doubtfully.

"I'm going to take it to school for show-and-tell," said Fawn.

"What are you going to tell about it?" said her mother.

"What a nice lamp it would make if it had a big lampshade," said Fawn.

"The bigger, the better," said her mother. "Now, go upstairs and start your homework. I'll be up to put supper on when I finish cleaning these combs."

"Okay," said Fawn. She thought about her Valentine's Day card—the special one. Should she ask her mom to mail it? What if her mom said, "Oh, honey . . ." and her voice just trailed off?

Fawn didn't have the nerve. She didn't take the card out of her knapsack. Instead, she said lightly, "Any mail from Daddy today?"

There was a pause. Then her mom said, "Oh, honey . . . not today." Her voice trailed off, and she didn't look at Fawn. She just kept sweeping up the dead curls on the floor.

Miss Earth's Broken Heart

When Miss Earth got home from school that day, her mother, Grandma Earth, was whipping up some Valentine's tarts in the kitchen behind Grandma's Baked Goods and Auto Repair Shop.

Miss Earth shucked off her parka and warmed her hands at the open oven door. "These are pretty," she said glumly, looking at the tarts.

"You don't sound like your usual blend of Shirley Temple–Florence Nightingale–Mary Poppins–Pollyanna," said her mother. "What's up, dear?"

"Valentine's Day makes me cranky," said Miss Earth.

Grandma Earth already knew that. She knew her darling daughter had been unlucky in love. She remembered when her daughter's fiancé had died, during the annual Macy's Thanksgiving Day Parade. The good man had been mowed down by a runaway Christmas float in Times Square. Santa Claus himself had jumped off his candy-cane throne and tried to administer first aid—oh, what a nightmare. Broadcast over national television! The famous news reporter, Meg Snoople, had been covering the parade for one of the major networks. She had burst into real tears and sobbed into her perky

14

fake-fur collar. The ratings had gone through the roof.

And the next year, Germaine Earth had taken a teaching job at the Josiah Fawcett Elementary School. Her students knew about the famous accident. But they didn't know the identity of their teacher's fiancé.

"I've made some extra tarts for your students," said Grandma Earth gently. "Just because you have a sad time at Valentine's Day, sweetheart, doesn't mean your students have to."

"Valentine's Day takes it out of me," said Miss Earth. She perched on a wooden stool and licked the beaters. "I do miss Rocco."

"Of course you do," said Grandma Earth. "No one ever said love was going to be easy."

Grandma Earth had only met Rocco Tortoni once, but she had approved of him. Eyes flashing with good humor. A patron of the arts, a devout baseball fan, a New York state senator. And a body right out of the Ab-Flab infomercials. Little children loved him. Old folks trusted him. Squirrels ate peanuts right out of his hand. Voters returned him to office.

Rocco Tortoni. Some had said he would be President Tortoni one day. Miss Earth would have been the First Teacher, dispensing pearls of wisdom at his side. And Grandma Earth would have been the First Grandma. She'd have set up a bakery in the basement of the White House, to raise a little extra money and help reduce the national debt.

Yes, Rocco had been a dream, a treasure, and now he was utterly dead. It was a shame.

There was a picture of him, a black-and-white photo

in a silver frame. It stood on the TV. He was smiling shyly. Miss Earth, who didn't approve of TV, sometimes sat and graded papers while her mother watched the medical drama shows. But when Miss Earth looked up from her work, she wasn't peeking at the TV. She was glancing at her dear departed Rocco Tortoni.

Though Grandma Earth knew this, she never remarked on it. Even grown daughters deserve their privacy. However, Grandma Earth wanted to have some real grandchildren one day, not just her daughter's students. So she had bought a cardboard cupid from the display rack at Clumpett's General Store to put her daughter in a thoughtful mood. The cupid was propped up against the phone book in the hallway.

"I'm going to run myself a bath and have a nice soak," said Miss Earth.

"Shall I ask Mayor Grass for dinner on Valentine's Day?" said Grandma Earth, blandly scrubbing the tart tins.

"Oh, Mama," said Miss Earth. "Really."

Grandma Earth knew this didn't mean *Really, go ahead.* But she pretended she misunderstood. When she had finished the washing up, she went to the telephone. There was a sack of little valentine hearts on the phone table, the pastel-colored type, with messages printed on them: BE MINE and LUV YA and KISS ME and EZ 2 LUV. The phone book was opened to the *G* page. There was Mayor Tim Grass's number. Next to the book, on the table, Miss Earth had arranged the hearts to spell out the word NO right below the paper cupid.

"Whoopsie," said Grandma Earth, sweeping the hearts onto the floor. "Oh, how clumsy of me. Oh, well. Now, let me get Timothy Grass on the phone, while my dear Germaine is upstairs, noisily running a bath."

♥

4

A Meeting of Matchmakers

The next morning, when Sammy Grubb tramped into the classroom, he had to hand it Miss Earth. Even though she wasn't thrilled with Valentine's Day, she didn't hold back. Her classroom was a festival of bulging red hearts and lacy doilies. True, it made Sammy feel sick, but he appreciated Miss Earth's professional zeal at classroom decoration, even though she personally thought that it was all sentimental garbage.

If there was one thing that Sammy Grubb worried about, it was being popular with the girls. *Too* popular. He liked all the girls in the class—more or less—he just hated being thought of as the Most Eligible Potential Boyfriend. Plenty of time for smoochy-woochy when he was grown up. For now, being the Chief of the Copycats Club took all his spare time.

As Sammy made his way to his desk, he noticed a new picture of a simpering cupid stapled to the bulletin board. Like a farmer sighting a greedy varmint raiding the seed bins, Sammy quickly lifted an imaginary bow and arrow, aimed down the shaft, released the string. "Kah-puuuhhhhh," he said softly. "You're history, baby."

"Oooh, Sammy's so *manly,* he can take potshots at

innocent flying infants," said Thekla loudly. She didn't mean it as a compliment. Sammy scowled and slid into his seat.

Thekla basked in the approving glances of her friends in the Tattletales Club. Since romance always made boys nervous, the week around Valentine's Day was a great time for girls to be alive. But deep down, Thekla wondered about herself. Were her classmates merely impressed by her, or did anyone like her enough to send her a card? Not just as part of the class assignment, but for real? Usually, like Sammy, Thekla tried to concentrate on running the club she was elected to govern. But every now and then her sharp little prickerbush of a heart trembled, unsure of itself. "Miss Earth, Sammy Grubb was shooting at your picture of a cupid," said Thekla suddenly. After all, she *was* a Tattletale.

"Thekla, stop picking on Sammy. And mind your own business. Cupids aren't an endangered species," said Miss Earth dryly. She added in a quieter voice, almost to herself, "Though it's certainly true that they haven't been seen around *here* for a while . . ."

When Miss Earth wasn't looking, Thekla stuck her tongue out at Sammy Grubb, just to let him know she still objected to him in principle. When she was done with this, she thought about Miss Earth's remark about the low population density of cupids in Hamlet, Vermont. Then she had a brilliant idea. As soon as Miss Earth's back was turned, Thekla imitated the whistle of the radiator to get everyone's attention. Then she made a circling motion with a single finger held up in the air, like somebody saying "Whoop-de-doo." It was the special sign for the Tattletales to have a meeting at the next available moment. The girls in the club nodded: Roger, gotcha, over and out. The boys shook in their seats. Tattletales were bad news in a dangerous season like this.

The first available moment for a meeting came at recess after lunch. On the playground, Thekla Mustard climbed to the top of a snowbank. The Tattletales gathered around her. Thekla said, "Girls, it's come to my attention that Miss Earth needs a new boyfriend. Who better than us Tattletales to pick someone out for her? The floor is open for nominations."

"Good idea, and seasonal besides," said Carly Garfunkel.

"How about Jasper Stripe, the janitor?" said Anna Maria Mastrangelo.

"No," said Thekla. "He watches *Court TV* every chance he gets, and Miss Earth doesn't like TV."

"What about Mr. Dewey, the town librarian?" said Sharday Wren.

"Possible. Bookish is good," said Thekla. "But his nose is always buried in his books. He might not notice Miss Earth's charms. Let's keep brainstorming."

"I know," said Nina Bueno. "Mayor Timothy Grass. He's not married."

"Hmm," said Thekla. "Maybe you've hit on it. Objections, anyone?"

Fawn Petros raised her hand. In her usual mild voice she said, "My mother does Widow Wendell's hair every Monday, and Widow Wendell tells her everything. I think Widow Wendell wants to marry Mayor Grass."

"Isn't Widow Wendell too old?" said Nina.

"*She* doesn't think so," said Fawn. "And how could somebody ever be too old for love?"

The Tattletales sighed in concert. What a shame to have to rule out Mayor Grass. He was a nice guy. He was good-looking without being dazzling, friendly without getting in your face about it. He was clever without being superior. He went around in comfortably worn chalk blue plaid flannel shirts all the time, too.

Lois Kennedy the Third said, "Miss Earth is first-class. She deserves a famous husband. What about that fellow who co-anchors on Meg Snoople's morning show, *Breakfast in America*? What's his name? Chad Hunkley? He's cute in a Royal-Canadian-Mounted-Police kind of way."

"He's a national newscaster," said Thekla shortly. "How could we get them to meet?"

Lois said, "Don't forget that when Meg Snoople came to Vermont in the fall, she interviewed me. I bet I could

get her on the line if I wanted to. I could arrange a meeting with Chad Hunkley." She snapped her fingers. Impressive. Thekla sensed another leadership challenge coming, and sighed. Sometimes she wished a comet would plunge out of the sky and smash Lois into the ground once and for all.

"Chad Hunkley and Miss Earth," said Anna Maria. "I like it. He could propose to her on the air. All America could watch over their cornflakes. Maybe the wedding could be on TV. We girls could be bridesmaids. We'd be famous."

The Tattletales loved that idea. But Mrs. Brill, the lunch lady, was ringing the bell. End of recess. Thekla hurried. "I have a perfect idea. For show-and-tell tomorrow I'll have Jasper Stripe wheel in the school's TV and VCR. I'll put on a tape of Meg Snoople's *Breakfast in America,* featuring Chad Hunkley. We can plant the idea in Miss Earth's mind, and plan our campaign from there. Agreed?"

"Miss Earth hates TV," said Lois. "You know that. She thinks it rots the brain and softens the muscles. Also it ruins your eyes."

"I'll pretend it's something educational," said Thekla. "Trust me, girls."

They did. Even Lois, who resented Thekla, had to trust her. Thekla was a person who got things done.

Across the schoolyard, Sammy Grubb finished up a snowball fight with his allies, the Copycats. They were pretending to be fierce warriors. But secretly each and every one of them was worried about that look in Thekla

Mustard's eye. They'd all known Thekla long enough to guess when she had a secret campaign brewing.

Mrs. Brill shouted, "Boys! I said *line up*!" She shook the bell furiously.

Pearl Hotchkiss, who didn't belong to the Tattletales or the Copycats, lined up with her classmates. She had her hands in her pocket. She could feel the wonderful card she had made for Sammy Grubb at home last night. It said:

> Love is love. Like is like.
> Love is scary. Like is not.
> Love is yucky. Like is lucky.
> Someone likes you <u>quite a lot</u>.
>
> A secret admirer

Pearl was proud of her cleverness. She'd typed the message on her father's computer and signed the signature with her left hand so her handwriting wouldn't give her away. Now, how to slip the note to Sammy tomorrow without him seeing her do it? She'd love to watch him open it up and glance around, trying to guess who sent it! Partly she hoped he wouldn't guess her. And partly she hoped he would.

♥ 5
Show-and-Tell

Friday was Valentine's Day. Fawn wrapped the Greek vase with a sweatshirt that said MY DAD WENT TO ANTARCTICA AND ALL I GOT WAS THIS LOUSY SWEATSHIRT. She tied the sweatshirt arms together and packed the whole thing carefully in her knapsack. On the school bus, she stuck the knapsack underneath her seat so nobody would kick it. When the bus pulled into the schoolyard and thirty-eight students catapulted out the doors, Fawn waited to be last. She didn't want to risk breaking that beautiful vase, not after it had come safely all the way from Greece.

Everybody in the Josiah Fawcett Elementary School was in a Valentine's Day fever. Even the principal, Hetty Buttle, read a valentine over the public address system. It went like this:

> On this day it's plain to see,
> You're the valentine for me!
> Just obey this simple rule:
> Even on Valentine's Day, no stampeding in the halls of the
> Josiah Fawcett Elementary School.

Principal Hetty Buttle wasn't good at making the lines of her poems the right length, but it was the thought that counted. From all over the school you could hear the sound of polite clapping. Seventeen kindergartners began to stampede down the hall to the office to tell the principal how much they loved her poem.

Miss Earth brought the strawberry tarts that Grandma Earth had made for the class. But the tarts were for later. First there was science, reading, lunch, show-and-tell, and math. Then: *party*.

Fawn couldn't wait until show-and-tell. She never had anything to bring except hair-care products from the Hamlet House of Beauty, or a postcard from Antarctica. This vase from Greece was the most exotic object she'd ever had the chance to show off.

The truth was that Fawn sometimes felt overwhelmed by school. Everyone else seemed so good at everything. Fawn was only so-so at reading. And math wasn't her strong point, either. In fact, she didn't seem to *have* a strong point, just a lot of weak ones. The other kids in the class weren't mean to her, but now and then they said things to make themselves look smart, which made her look smartless. Fawn didn't blame her classmates, but sometimes she wished she could impress them. Maybe today . . .

Of course, she hadn't thought about what she was going to *tell*, only what she was going to *show*.

After lunch Miss Earth said, "It's time for show-and-tell. Today it's Thekla, Fawn, and Mike. In alphabetical order, we'll start with Thekla."

Fawn hated alphabetical order. Thekla, who was so brainy, came right before her—Mustard before Petros—and Thekla always made her look dumb by comparison.

Thekla marched to the front of the room and said, "I would like to draw your attention to the TV monitor. This is a piece I recorded on Vermont Public Television about snowy owls. Since we study snowy owls in their natural habitat—Vermont—you should find this interesting. Afterward I will perform some owl calls." Thekla poked the videocassette in the slot and pressed the PLAY button. Miss Earth sighed and looked faintly cross. Show-and-tell wasn't supposed to come in a recorded segment.

They heard the *Breakfast in America* theme music—all drums and trumpets and synthesizer strings. The logo came flipping dizzily across the screen the way it did every morning, as snippets of famous American sights ran up and down the edges of the screen. Niagara Falls. The Rockies. The Statue of Liberty. The letters spelling Hollywood. "It's *Breakfast in America*!" enthused the announcer, who sounded as if he were crooning through a microphone drenched in maple syrup. "Starring your hostess with the mostest and a buttered piece of toastess—Meg Snoople! Reporting live later in the show from an active volcano in Hawaii!"

"This isn't Vermont Public Television," said Miss Earth.

"Just wait," said Thekla. "I taped over this. The owl part will start in a second. Patience."

"I have no patience for chat shows . . ." began Miss Earth.

"Shhhhhh," said all her students, except Salim, who in India had been raised to believe it was rude to *shhhhhh* a teacher.

"Also featuring anchorperson Chad Hunkley!" said the announcer. The credits showed handsome Chad Hunkley in khaki safari clothes, holding a microphone in his hand as he leaped toward a charging bull elephant.

"What a clunkhead," muttered Miss Earth.

"This morning our first report is by Chad Hunkley!" The announcer kept sounding as if he had never heard anything so exciting in his whole life. Well, Chad Hunkley was pretty gorgeous, you had to admit it. Even Fawn thought so.

The camera came in for a closeup. Chad Hunkley smiled as if trying to shatter the lens of the camera with the brilliant jags of his winning personality. "Hi, there, America," he said in a deep, whispery, closeup voice. "Ever wonder how those ladies in soap powder commercials get picked to show their dirty laundry to the nation? *Of course you have—*"

"Of course I *haven't*," said Miss Earth. "Thekla, fast-forward, please. We haven't time for this nonsense. The rest of America may eat this stuff up, but I'm allergic to trash."

"Oh, no! The fast forward is broken," said Thekla, pretending to press down on the button. "Well, just keep watching. By the way, isn't he a hunk?"

"He's a hunk, all right. A hunk of Swiss cheese with holes where his brains should be," muttered Miss Earth. All the Tattletales cast glances at one another. Miss Earth

27

often pointed out that sometimes kids tease each other to disguise the fact that they really *like* each other. Maybe she was just being rude about Chad Hunkley to conceal the truth that she really thought he was hot stuff.

"Notice those broad shoulders," said Thekla conversationally.

"The better to support such a swollen head, my dear," said Miss Earth.

"And, my, what a perfect smile," said Thekla.

"The better to distract you from his empty words, my dear," said Miss Earth.

"And those eyes, blue as cornflowers in a Vermont meadow in July!" said Thekla.

"They are mighty blue," admitted Miss Earth.

For a second, her guard was down. The Tattletales hoped that their plan was working.

But the boys broke the spell. "Oh, those eyes," said Sammy Grubb in a fluting voice.

"And those huge teeth! You know what they say: The bigger the teeth, the bigger the cavities!" said Forest Eugene Mopp.

"How 'bout those shoulders?" said Stan Tomaski. He pretended to swoon. "What a linebacker he would make. Miss Earth, why don't you marry that guy?"

The boys were breaking the spell, but they were also moving the subject forward. Thekla Mustard thought fast. "Well, how about it, Miss Earth?" she said. "Not such a bad idea."

"He *is* pretty good-looking," said Hector Yellow. The Copycats all stared at him. "Well, he is," Hector said again.

"Class," said Miss Earth, shaking her head, coming back to her senses. "I'd no more marry this noodlenik than I'd drink a milk shake made of mouthwash and motor oil. Thekla, you're wasting our time."

Miss Earth got up and pressed the OFF switch. "Sorry, Thekla," she said. "Tell us in your own words what you learned about snowy owls."

"They camouflage with the snow," said Thekla sullenly. "They go: *Whoo, whoo.* That's about all I remember."

"Come better prepared next time," said Miss Earth. Thekla sat down. All the girls in the class clapped for Thekla, except for Pearl, who yawned. The boys pretended to sob because gorgeous Chad Hunkley had disappeared from the TV screen.

"Fawn," said Miss Earth. "Your turn. Now, use your outside voice, not your mouse voice."

Fawn walked forward and set her knapsack carefully on the corner of Miss Earth's desk. She opened the knapsack and withdrew the sweatshirt.

"It's a vase from Greece," said Fawn in the biggest voice she could manage.

"Outside voice!" said everyone obnoxiously.

Fawn tried again. "A vase from *Greece.*" She untied the arms of the sweatshirt and slowly lifted the garment up. The vase was unveiled.

"Look at the craftsmanship!" said Miss Earth. "A Greek vase of this type is called an amphora, Fawn. Look at all those wonderful etched designs. What can you tell us about this amphora?"

"My aunt Sophia found it in a market in Athens," said

Fawn. "It has pictures of cupids on it, see? So I thought it would, like, be perfect for Valentine's Day." She pointed out the cupids. There were four of them. Each one was draped with a towel-like thing. Each held a bow and two arrows. There was some sort of writing beneath each cupid.

"Look," said Miss Earth. "Can you read this, Fawn?"

"I think it's Greek," said Fawn.

"Indeed it is," said Miss Earth. She had gone to a good teacher-training college where she had learned Greek, Latin, Spanish, French, Arabic, and a smattering of medieval Urdic-Finnish. So it was easy for her to trace out the four words that ran around the vase.

"Here, it says KOS," said Miss Earth. "This says NAXOS. This says MILOS. And this says RHODES. Do you know what they are?"

"Roads are what you drive on?" said Fawn.

"No, this is Rhodes, spelled differently. These are the names of four Greek islands in the Aegean Sea," said Miss Earth. "Kos, Naxos, Milos, and Rhodes. Fawn, what else can you tell us about this fascinating object?"

Fawn opened her mouth to speak, hoping that some interesting words would come out. Luckily, over the intercom, the principal's voice boomed into Miss Earth's classroom. "Excuse me, Miss Earth," said the voice of Principal Hetty Buttle.

"Yes," said Miss Earth, all pert and no-nonsense.

"Do you have the school TV and VCR in your room?"

"Yes, we have it, and we're through with it now," said Miss Earth.

30

"Good. The second graders need it. They're recording a Valentine's Day video message for their teacher, who's home with a broken leg. The children want to view their efforts so far. I can't send Jasper Stripe to get the TV and VCR because he's in the kindergarten, cleaning up a mess. The kindergartners had too much Valentine's Day candy, and they got overexcited in the stomach department."

"I understand," said Miss Earth. "Since children aren't allowed to push the cart with the TV and VCR on it, I will take it to the second-grade classroom myself."

"Thank you. Happy Valentine's Day, kids, and remember to floss," said Principal Hetty Buttle.

"She's in a jolly mood," said Miss Earth. "Now, Fawn, would you continue while I walk this down to the second grade? Tell your classmates about your Greek object of art." Miss Earth unplugged the TV and VCR, and she wheeled the audiovisual cart out the door.

"Well," said Fawn uncertainly. Even though she wanted her friends' approval, she hated having to be the center of attention to get it. "My aunt Sophia is really neat. Once she sent me a toy Trojan horse with little soldiers that fit inside."

"What's inside of this?" asked Forest Eugene.

"Nothing," said Fawn.

"Then why does it have a stopper all glued over?" asked Carly.

"To stop stuff from getting inside, I guess," said Fawn.

"Fawn, that's the stupidest jug I ever saw," said Thekla.

"Don't say *stupid*," said Pearl hotly. "Jugs can't be stupid." Pearl had her secret card for Sammy Grubb clutched in her hand. Any moment now, she'd nip forward and slip it in his desk . . .

"Fawn, it's my turn," said Mike Saint Michael. "Unless you have anything else to say." He pulled a butterfly net from the closet. "Look what I got for my birthday."

He leaped onto his desk. He held the net by the circular hoop and brandished the long handle like a sword. *"En garde!"*

"Look out!" cried Fawn.

The handle of the net caught one of the crooked handles of the vase. But Mike didn't notice. The vase soared up into the air. "No!" cried Fawn. Mike tried to turn the net around and catch the vase in midair.

While the kids jumped out of their seats, anticipating the crash, Pearl Hotchkiss pushed forward. There! She had stuck the card in Sammy's open backpack. And no one had seen a thing.

The vase slammed onto the corner of Miss Earth's desk. It shattered into several dozen shards. Clattering onto the linoleum floor, the puzzle pieces of vase left a cloud of reddish clay dust in the air. It was as if the inside space of the vase was still hovering, intact.

Then the reddish air began to swirl and sparkle. It twisted like a miniature sandstorm, like a bit of indoor weather.

"Fawn, I'm so sorry," said Mike. "I broke your amphora thingy."

"Look," cried Fawn.

The reddish air was dividing itself into misty, transparent shapes. The shapes grew denser and clearer by the moment. There were four of them, hovering with rapid wings just over the top of Miss Earth's desk. You couldn't quite make out what they were. Four bumblebees the size of gerbils?

The three smaller creatures clustered together in the air behind the fourth. Their wings made a buzzing sound. The fourth—the biggest one—flew forward a few inches. It opened its mouth and barked.

6

Four Stupid Cupids

The students in Miss Germaine Earth's class at the Josiah Fawcett Elementary School in Hamlet, Vermont, were, on the whole, rather well behaved. As students go. Generally they were quiet when possible, respectful of property, courteous to their elders. And why not? Since kindergarten they'd been well trained by a crop of good teachers. But on this Valentine's Day, when four buzzing bumblebee creatures materialized in the air before them, the students, quite simply, lost it. They all screamed as if the bloody heart of Frankenstein had just appeared before them.

In other classrooms up and down the corridor, heads of kids turned. Tongues of teachers clucked. As far away as the school office, Principal Hetty Buttle looked up from a heart-shaped box of Valentine's candy and pursed her lips disapprovingly. "Kids can be joys, but I can't stand the noise," said Principal Buttle to Mrs. Cobble, the school secretary.

"I think Miss Earth is away from the classroom, returning the TV and VCR," said Mrs. Cobble. "Any orange creams in there?"

"There's no excuse for sheer pandemonium," said Hetty Buttle. "Here, have a pecan cluster. I hate pecans." She popped the only orange cream into her mouth. She was the principal, after all.

In Miss Earth's room, the students had backed up against the cloakroom. The creatures buzzed in formation toward them threateningly. All the students could think about was being stung by a wasp the size of an artichoke. The Copycats and the Tattletales and Pearl Hotchkiss forgot about their usual reluctance to pal around together. They formed a huge shivering clump of terrified kid in the back of the room.

But the foremost of the buzzing shapes stopped a few feet away and peered at them. It yapped again. Thekla Mustard decided to die defending her fellow students. It would be good for her reputation. She detached herself from the crowd and marched forward. She looked more closely at the visitor.

"I don't believe it," said Thekla. "It seems to be a flying baby. It's barking at us. Everyone stand back—"

Sammy Grubb, not to be outdone by his rival, pushed ahead and interrupted Thekla. "It's sort of like the picture of that cupid on the bulletin board, only it doesn't look so simpery and idiotic."

A cupid cornering them *on Valentine's Day?* Most hearts felt faint. (But a few hearts leaped up hopefully.)

"Hail, cupid," stated Thekla, bristling with public importance. "We who are about to drop dead with fear salute you. Welcome. Take us to your leader, or are you the leader? Make yourself at home. *Mi casa es su casa.*"

The biggest cupid listened to Thekla. It cocked its ear and looked puzzled. It whimpered like a dog with a thorn in its paw.

"Awww," said Pearl Hotchkiss; she couldn't help herself. She had six younger brothers and sisters and was used to

taking care of whimpery little ones. "There, there. Don't be scared. Want us to sing you a song?" She couldn't think of any Valentine's Day carols except every romantic song she'd ever heard on the radio, and she hated all of them.

The cupid seemed puzzled. Then it began to zip around the room. It looked at the globe. It looked at the Valentine's Day decorations. It looked at the long strip of paper taped above the blackboard, on which the alphabet was written in cursive script. The cupid seemed to be reading the letters one by one. It got to *Z* and started over.

"We'll sing you that," announced Pearl. *"A-B-C-D-E-F-G . . ."*

The other kids joined in. *"H-I-J-K-LMNO-P. Q-R-S, T-U-V, W, X, Y and Z. Now you've learned your ABC's . . ."*

They paused. Forest Eugene, who was quick on his feet, concluded, *"Cupids, please don't sting us, please."*

The leader cupid buzzed the melody in a rather tuneless way, as if catching on. The other three cupids, who seemed smaller and more indistinct, buzzed along like backup vocalists. The children sang the alphabet song again. Then the lead cupid went and hovered before the banner of cursive script again, pausing in front of each letter.

"*A* is for *amphora*," said Thekla Mustard.

"*B* is for *broken* amphora," said Sammy Grubb, not to be outdone.

"*C* is for *cupids* from a broken amphora," said Pearl Hotchkiss.

"*D* is for . . . for . . ." said Fawn Petros, but she was too excited to think of anything.

"*D* is for *duuuhhhhh*," said Stan Tomaski. "Fawn, you're such a *dumbhead*."

The kids finished naming things in alphabetical order. The biggest cupid was a fast learner. It opened its mouth but didn't bark. It tried its new language. In a funny accent it squeaked, "*I* is for *I*?"

"Well, *I* is really for *me*," said Fawn, trying to be grammatical and not such a dumbhead.

"*I* sure isn't for *U*," said Moshe Cohn.

"Don't joke, you'll confuse it," said Sammy.

"I is confused," said the cupid, nodding. "I is surprised. I is a cupid. What is a *U*?"

"You are a cupid," said Sammy. "We are kids."

"Small goats?" said the cupid.

"Small humans," said Thekla. "Small, but smart for our age. Well, some of us are smart." She looked at Fawn and rolled her eyes. "*She* said nothing was inside the vase. Hel-*looooooooo*."

"Do you have names?" said Fawn, in as much of an outside voice as she could manage.

The bigger cupid flew up to the smaller ones. It tapped one of them on its head. "He named Milos." Of another, it said, "He named Naxos. Milos and Naxos is twins. Twins is sometimes nice to each other, sometimes not." The twins growled and smacked each other. Now that the cupids weren't as scared, their wings fluttered a little more slowly, and you could see their shapes better. They were starting to look less like bumblebees and more like dumpy little flying potatoes with human toddler faces carved in them.

The fourth cupid was even smaller than the twins—an infant. Its face was puckered up as if it wanted to bawl. The biggest cupid said, "This little baby? Named Kos. Milos, Naxos, and baby Kos. Is three boys, but not me boy. I is named Rhodes. I is the boss girl. But, please, you are calling me Rhoda."

"Hi, Rhoda," said Thekla. "You learn the alphabet fast."

"Is simple for cupids. Cupids smart," said Rhoda. "Even the English word *alphabet* is born from the first two letters in Greek: *alpha* and *beta*. So *A-B-C* and so on is easy."

"I'm getting dizzy," Fawn said. "Can you slow your wings down? You're hard to see. You're like humming-birds."

"I am being sorry," said Rhoda. Her voice was gentle but full of static. "I am needing to keep wings going or I am falling."

"Set yourself down on the desk," said Fawn.

"Oh," said Rhoda. "Good idea."

She aimed herself above the blotter on Miss Earth's desk and began to slow her wings. Gently she touched down. Milos and Naxos followed her lead but crash-landed in a couple of strawberry tarts. Little baby Kos whimpered, and Rhoda reached up and caught him out of the air and brought him down. The top of the desk was a mess of broken pastry and splashed strawberry filling. "Yum, yum," said Milos, who was plump, even for a cupid. Milos and Naxos began to fight over a piece of pastry.

"You stop that. You be good boys," said Rhoda warn-ingly. "Plenty food to go around."

The students came forward cautiously and surrounded

Miss Earth's desk. "How did you get in that vase?" said Fawn.

"We are having picnic," said Rhoda, then corrected herself. "We *were* having picnic. The boys were playing with their arrows. We saw a witch from Thessaly go by. The boys teased her. They made all the goats in neighborhood fall in love with her."

"How do you make goats fall in love with a witch?" said Thekla.

"I already told you, cupids are good at languages," said Rhoda. "We spoke sheepdog language. The boys barked like sheepdogs to round up the goats. I told the boys to stop, but they would not behave. Then they shot their magic arrows to make the goats fall in love with the witch. But the witch was clever and quick and she dodged the arrows, so she never fell in love with the goats. Then, *pazaam!* She enchanted us into this clay vase."

"Oh," said Sammy Grubb. "Why did you bark at us? Did you think *we* were goats?"

"We were in the dark for a long time," admitted Rhoda. "So we had ourselves a nap. Our eyes must take a little while to adjust to the light again. We are sorry for barking at you."

Baby Kos began to crawl toward Miss Earth's black vinyl pocketbook. He opened it and found a lipstick. "Mmmmm," he said, and took a bite.

"Kos is stupid," said Milos. "Kos, don't do like that. Do like this." Milos grabbed the lipstick and drew a heart on the side of Miss Earth's pocketbook.

"Kos is a *lot* of stupid," said Naxos. He grabbed the lipstick from Milos and added an arrow poking into the heart.

"Kos is just a baby," said Rhoda, in a voice that sounded as if she had said this a thousand times before. "Kos isn't stupid. He just doesn't know much yet. Boys, give me that paint stick. Oh, how I wish your mother never asked me to baby-sit you. Look at the mess you've made. Look at the mess we are in!"

Fawn said, "How long have you been in that vase? My aunt Sophia said it wasn't very old."

"I don't know. We've been asleep. But I do know this: A week ago my own mother shot an arrow at Alexander the Great."

Forest Eugene Mopp went to the dictionary to look up Alexander the Great and find out when he had lived.

Rhoda looked around the room. "Where are we?" she said. "This doesn't look like our land. Where are the sheep, the temples, the streams flowing with watery music? Where are my friends the naiads who live in the streams?" She flew up suddenly in a panic. "Where are the spirits of this place?" Without another word she dived toward the schoolyard, but she hit the glass of the windows with a rude thump.

"Ow," she said. "Hard air." She tried again.

"Stop, you'll brain yourself," said Fawn.

"It's window glass," said Sammy. "Don't you know about window glass?"

Rhoda felt the glass with her little pink palms. "It's a smooth carved slice of icy air," she said to the other cupids. "I can't get through it. It's like a wall made of invisible marble. We're trapped. What kind of nightmare place *is* this?"

She twisted her hands together as she gazed out the window. "There's nothing alive here!" she said. "Not a tree in leaf, not a patch of meadow in flower! No stream, no vine hanging heavy with grapes! No bees at their honey hives! Oh, friends, we are in no good place. We have been sent to Hades, where nothing can live."

"This isn't Hades," said Sammy Grubb, slightly offended. "It's New England, and proud of it."

Forest Eugene called from the reference table. "Hey, everybody, listen to this. Alexander the Third of Macedon, called Alexander the Great, lived more than twenty-three hundred years ago!"

"That was a long nap," said Thekla to Rhoda. "You

slept for two millennia and change. Have any good dreams?"

"Naxos snores in his sleep," said Milos.

"Milos drools in his sleep and makes nasty smells," said Naxos. They stuck their tongues out at each other, and bit each other on the elbows. Then they rolled around in the pastry like miniature sumo wrestlers.

Kos tunneled back into Miss Earth's pocketbook. He found the ignition keys to her Kawasaki 8000 motorcycle and dropped them in the pastry. Then he located a stamp and licked the gum off the back and stuck it on his own forehead. It was a LOVE stamp.

"Rhoda needs to think," said Rhoda, sounding desperate. "Boys, behave yourselves. Stop fighting and stop messing up."

The cupids fell silent. Miss Earth's students took this chance to look at them closely.

Rhoda sported a pink tunic with little white flowers embroidered on the hem. She fingered her skirt nervously and bit her lower lip. "Did we really nap for hundreds of years?" she said. "Oh, what a distance of time *that* is!"

Milos, the chunky cupid, wore a crimson cloth and a wreath of laurel leaves on his blond curls. "Milos didn't nap," he boasted. "Milos was just pretending."

Naxos had dark curls. He had a lavender tunic, and he carried a small harp with only four strings. He strummed the harp and sang like a bird—a sick little bird. *"A-B-C-D-E-F-G, H-I-I-I, I love me!"*

"Shh!" said Rhoda. "I am thinking."

Kos was swaddled in a yellow diaper. It was yellow

because the cloth was yellow, not for any other reason. Kos patted a lost mitten left on Miss Earth's desk as if it were a kitten, and lovingly said to it, "Me-*owwww*." Then he tried to pull it over his head.

Each of the cupids had a quiver belted across one shoulder, and each quiver held two arrows about three inches long. Were these the magic arrows that made goats fall in love with a witch? Could they make *persons* fall in love with each other? Or was that just a silly story from long ago?

Rhoda said to Miss Earth's students, "I needed to earn some coins to spend at the Pan-Athenian festival. So I agreed to baby-sit these cupids from next-door. Their mother wanted to take a few days of vacation on Mount Olympus. I didn't know that these boys would tease that witch and get us all locked up in vase. I never meant to leave our pleasant vale. And for so long! Do I have to baby-sit these boys for *eternity*?"

"Milos hopes not," said Milos. "You are too strict."

"Naxos hopes not," echoed Naxos. "You never let Naxos sing."

Kos found a powder puff and began to chew it as if it were a dusty pie.

"Don't worry," said Thekla. "It's better to be awake than asleep. Now you can go home."

"But which way is home?" said Rhoda. She looked out the classroom windows again. "Which way is our own motherland? We will fly ourselves there if we can break down this cold wall. Are we very far from Mount Olympus?"

Salim glanced out the window. Because the Josiah Fawcett Elementary School was built in the shape of a T, he could see across the snowy yard to the corridor that led from the office. Miss Earth was on her way back.

"You'd better hide," he said. "Our teacher's coming."

Immediately the four cupids began to zip around the room, crashing into the blackboard, the bookcase, the Valentine's Day bulletin board.

"Stop! Don't panic! You'll just make things worse!" cried Fawn.

"A teacher!" cried Milos.

"A teacher!" cried Naxos.

"We're doomed!" cried Milos. "What's a teacher creature?"

Kos tried to squeeze in the terrarium with Kermit the Hermit, but the frog gave the baby cupid such a dirty look that Kos backed off.

Mike Saint Michael took matters in hand. With his new butterfly net, he leaped on top of Miss Earth's desk and swooped the net sack around. Deftly he snared Kos from the terrarium table. He scooped Milos from the top shelf of the back cupboard, where the stout cupid was burrowing into someone's lunch. Naxos was trying to wrap himself in the flag; Mike unwrapped him.

Rhoda was harder to catch, as she was the most nervous. "Oh, we are being trapped again!" she cried.

"We'll protect you, Rhoda," said Fawn. "We won't let anyone hurt you. Trust us. Please."

"I can't!" screeched Rhoda. "I am getting in a tizzy!" She began to shriek and to toss her auburn locks. Then

44

she clapped her arms at her side and spun in the air with pinwheel frenzy. She rotated like the second hand of a clock going crazy at warp speed, around and around.

Mike lunged and bagged Rhoda in midair. Fawn stood ready with her knapsack open. One by the one the four cupids slid out of the butterfly net and into the knapsack. Fawn pressed her sweatshirt in on top of them to keep them quiet, and she latched the knapsack buckle. "Don't worry. You're safe," she said. "But no noise if you want to get home." The cupids stopped their wailing almost at once.

The door opened. Miss Earth walked in. There was Mike standing on her desk with a butterfly net in hand. His shoes were covered with strawberry jam and there were flakes of pastry crust all around him. Miss Earth's pocketbook had romantic graffiti on it, and its contents were strewn across the desk.

"Well," said Miss Earth, with uncustomary chilliness. "Show-and-tell continues. I can see what you've shown, Michael Saint Michael. Now would you mind *telling* me?"

Mike's mouth dropped open. Fawn felt sorry for him. She knew exactly how it felt when there weren't any useful words available. On the floor under her desk, her knapsack bulged and twitched a little. But luckily no one in there supplied any useful words, either.

Miss Earth canceled the party. Miss Earth had never known her students to be so ill-behaved. Miss Earth was shocked, *shocked, do you hear, shocked*. Mike Saint Michael tried to make up some excuse about an impromptu

Valentine's Day skit that had gotten out of hand, but Miss Earth would have none of it.

There was no fun and games. There were no strawberry pastries. Everyone passed out their valentines in silence. Thekla didn't get any cards from any secret admirers. Rats. The bloody valentine from Sammy Grubb got on her nerves, too. She stuck her tongue out at him.

"Thekla, watch that," said Miss Earth. "I'm in no mood today."

"I was just exercising my tongue—"

"Well, exercise your ability to keep your tongue in your mouth."

When Miss Earth wasn't looking, Sammy, daringly, mincingly, stuck *his* tongue out at Thekla. She opened her mouth to report him—once a Tattletale, always a Tattletale, after all—but thought better of it.

Fawn whispered to Pearl, "Thanks. That's a nice card."

A lot of the cards ended up in the trash basket at the end of the school day for the janitor to cart off to the Dumpster. Most did. But one didn't.

♥

7

Cupids in the Hamlet House of Beauty

When Fawn got off the school bus that afternoon, she ran into the Hamlet House of Beauty. Her mother was fussing over a touch-up on Widow Wendell, who was sitting under a hair dryer.

Widow Wendell was screeching. "Fluff up those spit curls, Gladys! I'm in a fighting mood. I'm not going to let Mayor Tim Grass go without a struggle. He may not be free for a meal tonight, but I'll snare him before long."

"Isn't he a bit young for you?" said Mrs. Petros loudly, over the noise of the hair dryer.

"Who's counting? I'm an old bird," cawed Widow Wendell, "but a plucky one. I've made up my mind. Now I just have to make up his."

"Hi, dear," said Mrs. Petros to Fawn. "How did show-and-tell go?"

"Well," said Fawn, "Aunt Sophia's vase bit the dust."

"No," said Mrs. Petros. "How awful. Still, it was pretty ugly."

"Who you calling ugly?" yelled Widow Wendell.

Mrs. Petros gestured; Widow Wendell craned her

head. "Oh, hello there, Fawn," she said. "I don't think Fawn's so ugly, Gladys."

"Never mind," yelled Mrs. Petros.

"I hear she's not very bright, though," said Widow Wendell.

Mrs. Petros flipped off the hair dryer. Widow Wendell's silver-blue hair looked like a slightly smaller version of the hair dryer helmet itself: crisp, lacquered, impervious to attack. Mrs. Petros surveyed her handiwork and said, "Mabel Wendell, don't you make remarks about my daughter. She's bright enough, and kind and good, too."

"Well, I didn't mean anything personal," said Widow Wendell, pouting. "We can't all be Einstein's Little Helper."

"That'll be fourteen fifty," said Mrs. Petros in a steely voice.

"It was twelve fifty the other day," said Widow Wendell.

"I'm charging two bucks extra for the insults to my daughter's intelligence," said Mrs. Petros.

Widow Wendell paid and stalked off in a huff. She didn't leave a tip.

"Mom," said Fawn, "it's okay. I know I'm not the brightest banana in the bunch."

"Dearie," said her mother, "you have to stop being so down on yourself. You do your best. And everyone has a different strength. Growing up and being happy is a matter of finding out what your strength is and developing it. I can't do calculus, but give me a little styling gel and I can make the mummy from the tombs of Giza look like a movie star. Your father isn't so great at family affairs, but he's the world expert on penguin relations."

To change the subject, Fawn said, "I wish Daddy would come home."

Mrs. Petros put down her broom and hugged her daughter. "Honey, there's no connection between how smart you are and where Daddy is. I wish that he could live here, too. But there aren't any penguins in Vermont. Besides, you know how much he loves you."

"I know," said Fawn sadly. It was the afternoon of Valentine's Day, and the special valentine she'd made—for her dad—was still in the knapsack. She hadn't had the nerve to send it to him, mostly because she could imagine him not even noticing that she *hadn't* sent one. "He loves me, I know," said Fawn. "He just loves penguins more."

Mrs. Petros blew her bangs out of her eyes and tried again. "Tell me about your school day."

Fawn suddenly remembered the cupids in her knapsack. How could she be so stupid! Once the class had settled down to schoolwork again, Fawn had forgotten about the cupids. "Gotta go start my homework," said Fawn.

"You have all weekend," said her mom.

"Sooner I start, sooner I'm done," said Fawn. She grabbed her knapsack and bounded up the stairs to the apartment above the shop.

"My last customer of the day is Grandma Earth, who's in here for a wash-and-dry at four o'clock," called Mrs. Petros. "I'll be up after that."

"Gotcha," Fawn yelled down the stairs, and slammed the door of her bedroom.

She set the knapsack on the bed and opened it up. The cupids came out in a flutter of wings and reddish dust. "There you are!" said Fawn. "I'm sorry to have left you squished and scared in there. Especially after you'd been cooped up in the vase all that time."

Rhoda looked warily at Fawn as if she wasn't sure Fawn could be trusted. "Keep us captive if you must," she said. "But be decent about it. The boys are hungry. Do you have any olives and bread, some fish with lemon, some spinach, or some feta cheese?"

"How about peanut butter on crackers?" said Fawn.

"Yes!" said Milos. "Poor Milos wants peanut butter! What's peanut butter?" He clapped his hands in excitement.

"Crackers!" said Naxos. "What's crackers?" He strummed his harp and sang, *"A-B-C-D-E-F-G, no one eats as much as me!"*

Kos found a red velvet scrunchie of Fawn's and began to pet it. Then he tried to stick the tip of his bow into the electrical outlet. "Stop, you'll fry yourself!" cried Fawn. "Rhoda, watch them." Kos began to cry, and he snuggled up under Rhoda's wings.

Rhoda was looking at Fawn's bedside lamp. The wooden base was painted like a clown face topped with red yarn hair. The lampshade was supposed to be its hat. "Who's this, the spirit of your dwelling place?" said Rhoda.

Fawn pulled the string. The light bulb went on. The clown leered brightly at them. The cupids screamed in terror. It sounded like four chipmunks being sucked down a sewer drain. Luckily, Mrs. Petros was running the water downstairs so she didn't hear a thing.

"It's all right," said Fawn. "It's not alive. Chill, will you?" She left them for a minute.

When she came back with the peanut butter, Milos and Naxos were fighting over whose turn it was to swing on the cord and turn the clown on or off. Rhoda was muttering, "Amazing. It's like your own private sun god here in your room. Even if it's a stupid-looking sun god."

"Don't say *stupid*," said Fawn, who found that word uncomfortable since it was so often applied to her. "Say *unusual*."

"Peanut butter is unusual," said Rhoda, tasting it. She wrinkled her nose. But the boy cupids tried it—and liked it. Naxos and Milos couldn't talk for a while, because the peanut butter had stuck their mouths shut. Rhoda remarked, "If I could serve them peanut butter now and then, I could have some quiet time to think. Naxos and Milos are too talky. Now. That old witch of Thessaly locked us in a clay prison. You have freed us, but we are still imprisoned in our new liberty. We don't know where we are, or if you will help us get home."

"I'll try," said Fawn. "But meanwhile we must be very careful. Nobody should know about you who doesn't already. Do you know what they'll do to you if they discover you?"

"No," said Rhoda. "What?"

"I don't know," Fawn admitted. "Something bad. Maybe put you on the TV news, make you famous and public. That's another kind of prison, I think. Awful. But I'll protect you from that. First, tell me something. How could you learn English so quickly?"

"Cupids can learn any language quickly," said Rhoda. "They have to, because cupids bring love, and love is everywhere. Is this English I am speaking?"

"Yup."

"So we are not in Greece? Are we in Englandia? Englesburg? Englistan? What do you call this place?"

"We're in America," said Fawn.

"Why aren't we speaking Americish?"

"I don't know," said Fawn. "There isn't any such thing."

"But where is Greece?" said Rhoda.

Fawn got her father's old globe. "See, here's Greece, and then you go across Europe this way—here's England, and Scotland, and Ireland, and Iceland, and Greenland . . . all the way over here to North America."

Rhoda looked doubtfully at the globe. She petted the white jagged shapes of peninsular Greece and its hundreds of islands. She sniffed it. "Where is the good earth smell of wild oregano, and wheat, and sheep droppings?" she said. She put her ear down to the globe. "I do not hear the rushing sound of mountain streams, nor my girlfriends the naiads, the spirits of the streams, singing their watery odes." She put her eyeball almost against the painted tin of the globe. "I do not see that nasty witch, nor the broad shoulders of Mount Olympus. You are stupid. This is not Greece. This is a hollow ball painted with shapeless features."

Fawn said, "It *means* Greece."

Rhoda sniffed. "It doesn't know *how* to mean Greece."

Fawn tried again. "It's only an *idea* of Greece. Really, you are in Vermont in the good old U.S. of A. I'll show you. Here's a road map of the whole country." She spread it out. Rhoda glanced at it witheringly as if were nothing more than a colored paper carpet. Then something caught her eye. "Look," she said. "Here's an Athens and a Sparta. And a Corinth and an Ithaca and a Syracuse. All those names of Greek places! Someone has stolen our names. If this is a picture of America, then Greeks must have colonized America."

"No," said Fawn, trying to remember some history. "The Native Americans were here first, and then the Pilgrims came."

"Where are they coming from? Pilgrimland?"

"No, that sounds like a theme park," said Fawn. "I forget where the Pilgrims came from."

Rhoda said, "If we are speaking English, *someone* must have come here from England."

Fawn went back to the globe. "Look. The U.S. is here. England is here. Greece is here."

"What's down here?" said Rhoda, looking below. "Something white leaked out of the bottom of your ball. Does it need a diaper change?"

"That's Antarctica," said Fawn. "It's a place."

"What do they speak there?" said Rhoda.

"Penguish," said Fawn.

"This is interesting," said Rhoda. "But I still think this looks like a badly painted toy ball, not a place. I want to go back to Greece. Can you take us there?"

"Now?" said Milos. "With a peanut butter snack to eat before we go?"

"Now!" said Naxos, strumming a hopeful sort of chord on his harp.

Fawn looked at them hopelessly. She didn't know how to explain to them about distance. Greece wasn't as far as Antarctica, but it was still too far to walk. But before she could think of a new way to say it, Rhoda clapped her hands on her mouth. "Oh, the love of Zeus!" she said. "I completely forgot the rules."

"What rules?" said Fawn.

"Since you freed us, we must do you a favor before we can go home," said Rhoda. "The only favor we know how to do is romance. Do you want someone to fall in love with you? We can arrange it."

"No way. I'm only a kid," said Fawn. "Are you nutso?"

Rhoda took the arrows out of her quiver. "Each of us has two arrows," she said. "When we were captured, we had only these left. It's so easy to shoot a couple of human creatures with a pair of arrows. Then both will fall in love with each other."

"Wow," said Fawn. "Does it really work?"

"Yes," said Rhoda. "But I don't want to waste any arrows. We can't get any more until we get home. The arrows are made from cypress wood from the sacred grove on Mount Olympus."

"Amazing," said Fawn. She was beginning to have an idea. "My friends the Tattletales are trying to help our teacher fall in love with a TV announcer. Could you arrange that?"

The three boys looked eager. Even Kos began to finger his bow. Rhoda said uneasily, "Maybe we need a little target practice first. After all, it's been so long . . ."

"No," said Milos. "Milos just needs food first, for strength. Then: Presto! We take turns, and it's Milos's turn. You know it is!"

Naxos added, "Once Naxos learns a skill, Naxos doesn't forget it." He sang, *"A-B-C-D-E-F-G, no one's a better archer than me."*

"Good," said Fawn. "I'll call Thekla Mustard, and we'll have a meeting of the Tattletales and make our plans. If you can help us, we'll try to see that you all get home at last."

"We'll do our best," said Rhoda. "But I don't want to be locked in a ball of colored tin. That's not home to me." She gave the globe a little kick.

Kos nodded and began to suck on his toes. He sat back on the knapsack for warmth. The Valentine's card Fawn had made for her dad slid out of the knapsack. Fawn almost said, "Could you cupids make my dad love

my mom and me enough to come home to live with us?"
But she didn't think even cupids could manage that.

At four twenty Fawn's mother came upstairs. She was surprised to find Fawn in her bedroom with the door closed. "Fawn," she called, "you can take a break from your homework. You have all weekend to finish it. Meanwhile, do you want to go tidy up the salon for me? I've got to endorse today's checks and write up the bank deposit slip."

"Okay," said Fawn.

"We'll come, too," whispered Rhoda. "Don't leave us alone."

Fawn wasn't so sure about this idea, but she let the cupids clamber into the knapsack. Her mother's head was bowed over the pocket calculator as she pored over a small pile of checks. She didn't see Fawn flash by with her knapsack on her back. "Give a good scouring to the sinks, too, honey," said Mrs. Petros. "We'll have frozen pizza for supper tonight as a treat."

The shop was shut and the CLOSED sign hung in the door. Only a few cars went by—commuters returning from Dartmouth College, locals doing some last-minute shopping at Clumpett's General Store, parents picking up their kids from ballet class at the Flora Tyburn Memorial Gym. The cars zipped by too fast for anyone to look in and see some cupids on the loose.

Fawn turned on the radio so her mother wouldn't hear the cupids. Syrupy Valentine's Day songs oozed out. "Oooh, what's that noise?" said Rhoda.

"It's music," said Fawn.

"Hah, call that music?" said Rhoda. "It sounds like an anemic thunderstorm being played by limp, lazy clouds who aren't up to the task."

The cupids liked the salon at first. Kos found a yellow duck in the toy box and rode it, squeaking, up and down the counter. Milos and Naxos took turns jumping off the back of the haircutting chair into the bin of swept-up hair clippings. Rhoda sat on the top of the cash register with her feet in the open change drawer, kicking the pennies.

Fawn knew the ropes here. It was easy. Spray the mirrors with ammonia cleanser and wipe them down; sweep the floor; empty the trash baskets; line up the clean combs and scissors on the wheeled tray; fill in the spaces if anyone had bought some luxury hair care products (but no one ever did). She did all this, then turned her attention to the deep sink. She dusted it with blue powder and rubbed hard on the bottom and sides. Rhoda flew over to watch.

"A hard-walled box without a lid," she said.

"Called a sink," said Fawn, puffing with the effort. "It's for washing hair." She pulled out the hose and pressed the lever to rinse out the suds. Rhoda looked delighted.

"A stream!" she said. "Do that again!"

When Fawn obliged, Rhoda's face fell. "Oh, it's a stupid stream. There are no naiads here. It's just dead water. There's no spirit to it at all."

"It has three speeds," said Fawn, demonstrating. "Can get hot or cool."

"I want to go back upstairs," said Rhoda. She collected

Kos from the toy box and looked sternly at the twins, who were having a log-rolling competition in the other sink, using some hair curlers. "This is a beauty salon? There's no beauty here. Nothing is real."

Fawn shrugged. "Sorry. I'm almost done. Look, don't be sad. I'll, like, sneak you some frozen pizza tonight for a treat."

"Even the food is frozen here," said Rhoda. "This *is* Hades."

8

Roses and Regrets

That same afternoon, Miss Earth passed the office on her way out of the school. Principal Hetty Buttle was busy with file folders. She looked up to wave at Miss Earth and say, "How was your classroom's Valentine's Day party, Germaine?"

Miss Earth said, "Never happened. The children were jumpy. Frankly, I'm glad it's Friday."

"Any plans for the weekend?" said Principal Hetty Buttle.

"Mercifully, no," said Miss Earth. "I'm worn out. I think I'll just go home and have dinner with my mother. Maybe I'll start the latest book by Stephanie Queen. It's a suspense thriller called *Mauled in Manhattan*. Killer crocodiles get loose in the Manhattan sewers. They terrorize the populace, and then they begin to hijack subway cars."

"Sounds like a romp," said Principal Hetty Buttle. "I'd like more time to read. But I have too many reports to the school committee."

"By the way," said Miss Earth, "what's the blow-up doll in the corner?" A life-size balloon figure was bobbing gently between the file cabinet and the word processor.

"Don't you recognize him? It's Cap'n Truheart," said

Principal Hetty Buttle. "You know, from the afternoon TV show. I tape the show and watch it on the weekends. It's pure junk. I adore it. So I was buying my old dad some Valentine's candy over in Hanover yesterday, and I won this balloon by being the one-thousandth customer of the day. I accepted my prize because I thought the kindergartners might like Cap'n Trueheart. Alas, they didn't. They all threw up their Valentine's candy."

"Sometimes TV makes me want to throw up, too," said Miss Earth. "I prefer to spend my time with realistic fiction, like *Mauled in Manhattan*."

"Well, enjoy your book," said Principal Buttle. "I'm sure Cap'n Trueheart would be a little bit more interesting himself if he ever read a word."

Both of them laughed. The balloon figure of Cap'n Trueheart looked as if he'd never even heard of the concept of a book. His big blue eyes and painted knob of a chin had the smooth and perfect look of a TV personality unblemished by actual life experience.

On the way home Miss Earth imagined what a nice evening she would have. She and her mom could order some takeout food from the Mango Tree, the store that Salim Bannerjee's dad ran. Grandma Earth would set a batch of bread dough to rise and then watch TV. Miss Earth would insert her earplugs and settle down in the chair near the good lamp. She liked Spangles O'Leary, the heroine of the Stephanie Queen books. Spangles O'Leary was such a cutup!

When Miss Earth parked her Kawasaki 8000 Silver Eagle motorcycle in the driveway, her mother came to the garage door and said, "Sweetheart, I need some black olives. Do you mind running over to the Grand Union supermarket?"

"I thought we'd order out, as we usually do on Friday nights," said Miss Earth.

"No, I'm making a special treat," said Grandma Earth.

Though Miss Earth was tired, she was good-natured. "I see you've had your hair done. Nice," she said. Then she went to the Grand Union. Once there, she rolled her eyes at the displays of Valentine's candy—big fat red boxes of chocolates! Wrapped with red silk bows! Every cashier was wearing red. This was the usual color of the store uniform, but today it seemed annoying. Miss Earth didn't approve when the cashier winked at her and said, "Have a romantic evening, Miss Earth!"

Miss Earth thought, What did the cashier mean by *that*?

She soon found out. By the time she got home, Grandma Earth had closed up the shop for the day and was busy bustling in the kitchen. Shallots sizzled aromatically in olive oil. "You're fussing," said Miss Earth.

"Oh, well," said Grandma Earth in a high voice. "Once a year, why not?"

The doorbell rang. "Would you get it, Germy?" said her mother, using an old pet name to which Miss Earth usually refused to answer.

On her way to the front door, Miss Earth passed through the dining room. The table was cleared of newspapers, bills, recipes, and grocery store coupons. It was set with three of the unchipped plates. A pair of candles stood in blue glass candlesticks. "Whatever is going on?" asked Miss Earth.

She threw open the door. On the doorstep was Mayor Timothy Grass.

"Tim," said Miss Earth suspiciously. "What are you doing here?"

He drew a bunch of roses from behind his back. "Happy Valentine's Day."

"Mom!" bellowed Miss Earth. "You have company."

Grandma Earth came bustling from the kitchen, wiping her hands on her apron. "Oh, Tim, so glad you could come for dinner," she cooed.

"For dinner?" said Miss Earth.

"The flowers are for both of you," said Mayor Grass.

"How silly," said Miss Earth. "Well, don't stand there on the doorstep. Do you think we want to heat the entire state of Vermont in February?"

Mayor Grass came in. He removed his hunter's cap. His balding head gleamed a little in the overhead hallway light. He shucked off his red plaid lumberjacket. Underneath he was wearing his best sweater-vest, the one that had a pattern of cows marching back and forth across it. "I was glad to be invited for dinner," he said. "I don't like to eat alone on Valentine's Day."

"Well," said Miss Earth, who had been trying to forget it was Valentine's Day, "I suppose everybody has to eat somewhere. Though Valentine's Day sometimes causes me to lose my appetite."

"Aren't you going to ask our guest to sit down?" said Grandma Earth.

Miss Earth blushed. She tried to regain her good manners. "I'm sorry. I've had a difficult day. And Valentine's

Day is not easy for me. I thought I'd just come home and read a good book. Perhaps if I go take an aspirin, I'll feel better."

"I brought you a pincushion, too," said Mayor Grass, pulling it out of his pocket. It was red and heart-shaped. He held it out to Miss Earth, who stared at him so crossly that he changed the subject. "What're you reading, Germaine?" he stammered. "Is that the latest Stephanie Queen?"

Miss Earth said, "Well, yes, as a matter of fact, it is."

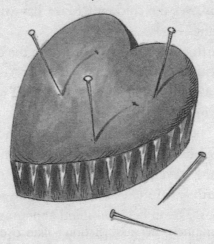

"I like Stephanie Queen myself," said Mayor Grass. "At Christmas I read *Helpless in Hollywood*, and before that I really enjoyed *Ballistic in Baghdad*, where Spangles O'Leary single-handedly brings an end to the Mother of All Wars."

"I'm not much of a reader," said Grandma Earth. "I tried *Senseless in Seattle*, but I couldn't get through it. I'm going back to finish my cooking. Germaine, offer our guest a drink."

Miss Earth followed her mother to get some root beer. "Mother, you have a lot to answer for," she muttered. "I told you I didn't want to have dinner with Mayor Grass on Valentine's Day. I'm not at all interested in him. And how does the whole town know? The cashier at the Grand Union made a smart-alecky remark."

"I heard through the grapevine that Widow Wendell invited Mayor Grass for dinner tonight, and he told her he *had a date*," said Grandma Earth, sprinkling capers and brown sugar over the chicken. "Make hay while the sun shines, darling."

Miss Earth poured the root beer into the glasses with such ferocity that it fizzled onto the tray. "If you don't watch out, Mama, I'm going to take myself upstairs and lock myself in my room!"

"I may be old, but I'm still your mother," said Grandma Earth. "Now, you march in there and chat with our guest, and leave the rest to me."

Miss Earth was furious. She hated to be set up. As if she couldn't make up her own mind about matters of the heart! Into the parlor she carried the tray with two glasses of root beer on it. Mayor Grass had jammed the roses into a milk-glass pitcher he'd found in the hall, and the pitcher took up the coffee table, so Miss Earth looked around for where she could set down the tray.

The top of the TV was clear. She began to head over to it, when she realized what was missing.

Her black-and-white photo of Rocco Tortoni. It had been tidied away.

Miss Earth managed to keep from bursting into tears.

She set the tray down and said gently, "Help yourself, Tim. I'll be back in a moment. I should put water in this vase so the roses don't . . . don't . . . die . . ."

Then she walked with dignity up the stairs to her bedroom. She closed the door quietly and sat down on her bed. She wanted to weep, as she had wept so many nights before. But all she felt inside was cold, and calm, and a little bit dead.

9

The Sting of a Cupid's Arrow

Saturday morning was a busy time at the Hamlet House of Beauty. Mrs. Petros and her weekend assistant, Hank McManus, were lathering up a storm. The girls of the Tattletales Club said hi and tramped through the shop to the apartment overhead. They draped their coats and hats over radiators, and gathered around the kitchen table. Thekla perched herself on the counter like a big shot.

"Carly, Sharday, Anna Maria, Fawn, Nina, and Lois," said Thekla Mustard. "And, of course, *me,* the Empress of the Tattletales. So everyone is accounted for. Good. Now, Fawn, I yield the floor to you. You called us here. You have to take charge."

Fawn didn't want to take charge. But the cupids were her guests. So she drew a deep breath and murmured, "Where to start?"

"At the beginning, dummy," said Anna Maria.

"Don't call me dummy," said Fawn. "I'm not dumb."

"Fawn, Anna Maria was just using an *expression,*" said Thekla. "Shall I take over the meeting, then, if you don't know where to start?"

"The cupids are Fawn's," said Lois, who loved to needle the Empress of the Tattletales. "So don't get snippy, Thekla."

"The cupids aren't actually *Fawn's*," said Sharday. "I mean, you can't own a cupid."

Fawn ran her tongue over her braces and tried to think of how to start. "Anybody want a glass of water?" she blurted out.

"Focus, Fawn," said Thekla. "Or I'm going home."

"Well, it's the cupids," said Fawn. "They said they can help us, but also they're asking if we will help them. They can shoot their arrows and make people fall in love."

There was a moment of silence. None of the Tattletales wanted to be in love, especially with any of the Copycats. The girls just liked to frighten the boys with threats of love. It was so much fun to be overwhelming. Even if you just batted your eyelashes, you could make boys turn pale with terror.

Then Thekla broke the mood and said, "Fawn, start from the beginning. I need to get this straight. This is fabulous. If what they say is true, *wow*! Talk about your ultimate secret weapon."

"Rhoda, the girl cupid, told me that they could make pairs of people fall in love. Those little arrows can 'sting' people into romance. Rhoda could shoot one arrow at, say, Jasper Stripe the janitor, and another arrow at, say, Mrs. Brill the lunch lady, and the janitor and the lunch lady would, like, fall in love with each other."

Thekla said, "Go get those cupids and let me talk to them."

"They don't want to come out," said Fawn. "Frankly, they're sort of scared of Vermont. It's not much like Greece. And it seems very cold to them. They would rather stay in the little nest I've made for them so they can keep warm. Besides, Rhoda is reading my picture books to bone up on her English. She's shy about not knowing it perfectly yet."

"That's stupid," said Thekla. "She's a new immigrant. She can't help being bad at English."

"Rhoda said they would be happy to follow our instructions. But when they've done what we ask," said Fawn, "they want to be sent home. To Greece. And I've promised that we'll help them get there."

"And so we shall," said Thekla. "One good turn deserves another. Especially if we can use these arrows to sting the Copycats. We could sting Sammy Grubb and make him fall in love with Principal Buttle. Wouldn't that be rich." She laughed in her why-not-conquer-the-world way.

"Or we could make Sammy Grubb fall in love with Pearl Hotchkiss," said Nina. "Sometimes I think Pearl might have a crush on Sammy already."

"Treachery is wonderful," cried Thekla. "What fun to be troublesome."

"We can't ask the cupids to be *troublesome*," said Fawn crossly. "We must be thoughtful and kind. If we're going to help Miss Earth out, let's sting *her* and then we could, like, sting Chad Hunkley on the videotape."

"Fawn," said Thekla. Her mouth dropped open. She spoke slowly, as if astonished. "Fawn, Fawn, Fawn. Let me say it again: *Fawn*."

"What?" said Fawn. "What, already? What what what?"

"You are a genius," said Thekla.

Fawn beamed.

"This doesn't mean you're always a genius in *everything,*" added Thekla.

Fawn knew *that.* If she were so smart, she'd figure out how to get her father home.

"Enough is enough. We don't mind how the cupids talk. Let's confirm our acceptance of their kind offer. Tell Rhoda to come out here," said Thekla. She raised her voice. "Rhoda? It's the Empress of the Tattletales speaking."

"We're busy," called Rhoda's voice from Fawn's bedroom. "Milos is playing kick the world with that tin ball. Naxos is singing songs of praise about himself. Kos is trying to wriggle into a sock and use it as a sleeping roll. And I'm reading. We'll come out when it's time to help you, but not before. Besides," said Rhoda, "it's *cold* in Vermont. I still think this is Hades. No naiads singing their music that sounds like water running over the stony path of a streambed!"

"Well, it *is* winter," said Thekla huffily, as if she had invented winter herself, and felt she was being insulted on how cold she had made it.

"This is Vermont," said Rhoda. "I like Greece. I miss it." Her voice got sad, and she stopped talking. They all heard the sound of a page turning.

The Tattletales got ready to go. They hunched themselves into parkas and stamped their feet into their boots. They burrowed their hands into mittens and pulled knitted caps down over their ears. They were chattering up a storm. What kind of bridesmaid's gowns could they wear

to the wedding of Miss Earth and Chad Hunkley? Would they be long and flowing, ribboned and laced? The colors of spring: pink, rose, lilac, fern, a delicious pale yellow? Maybe Anna Maria Mastrangelo could sing a song from the altar. Maybe Sharday Wren could do a little interpretive dance. Maybe Thekla Mustard could get permission to be a temporary justice of the peace and perform the ceremony herself!

The girls tramped down Tyburn Road toward the center of town. Fawn, waving good-bye, was thinking: Maybe we'll be able to get these little cupids home. Everyone should get to go home. Distant dads and little cupids both.

Fawn's dad was more distant in space—Antarctica was farther than Greece. But the poor cupids' mothers were more distant in time. Would the mothers even still be there?

As Lois Kennedy the Third peeled off from the group, heading up Squished Toad Road, she was thinking: So maybe that cupid Rhoda shoots a pair of arrows at Miss Earth and Chad Hunkley. Lovey-dovey time. Great. But there will *still be three sets of arrows left.*

One set could be used to sting Thekla Mustard and Sammy Grubb. Thekla might make a royal fool of herself, tossing her heart at Sammy! The other Tattletales would vote her out of office. And they'd vote Lois Kennedy the Third *in.* Finally Lois would get to be Empress, after all these years of waiting.

♥
10

The Sting of Milos

By Sunday, Miss Earth had forgiven her mother for trying to set her up with Mayor Grass. "It's not that I don't like him," said Miss Earth, when she and her mother had returned from nine o'clock mass at Saint Mary in the Tombstones. "Timothy Grass is a nice man. I've known him forever. When I was a teenager and my bike got a flat tire, he fixed it for me. He had just graduated from Saint Michael's College outside Burlington."

"You realize that he's not so much older than you," said Grandma Earth, setting out some doughnuts on a plate and putting the weekend edition of the *Hamlet Holler* on the table. "What's eight or ten years when love is at stake?"

"There you go again," said Miss Earth. "Listen to me, Mother."

"Oh, when you start dragging out *Mother*, I know I'm in trouble," said Grandma Earth.

"It embarrasses me to talk about this," said Miss Earth. "But you have to understand. I'm not sure that I'm capable of falling in love again. Too much of my heart remembers my dear Rocco. Besides, I'm happy with my job, my students, and living here with you. Happiness comes in many varieties, of which being married is only one."

"Don't I know it," said Grandma Earth with gusto. "Put me up to my elbows in a Dodge Valiant with a blown valve cover gasket, and I think I've died and gone to heaven."

"So you'll stop pestering me about Mayor Grass?"

"Honey," said her mother, "do you remember when you were little and you wouldn't eat your vegetables? I told you to try them, try them once. Vegetables are an acquired taste. For some people, so is love."

"I grew to love broccoli," Miss Earth admitted. "But I never asked broccoli to love me back. For true love to work, it takes two. And I'm just not up for the effort of being sure about Mayor Grass's feelings for me. He's sweet and kind, but what does that mean? Let's just leave it alone. Please."

"I could find out for you," said Grandma Earth.

"Mother," said Miss Earth sharply. "Do you want the comics or the sports section, or would you rather I hit you over the head with a frying pan?"

"I'll take the comics," said Grandma Earth.

They ate their doughnuts in silence.

Across town, Sammy Grubb climbed into his treehouse. It was freezing cold, but Sammy warmed up by pushing all the snow off the floorboards and shaking the icicles off the limbs of the tree. He wasn't sure he wanted to call a meeting of the Copycats. It was too embarrassing. When he had opened his knapsack to get out the books for his homework, he had found a note there. A note from a secret admirer. *Someone likes you quite a lot,* it had said. Now, there were words to strike fear into the heart of any boy! Sammy was proud of being the Chief of the Copycats. He didn't want to admit to being scared. What if the note came from Thekla Mustard?

He thought of that look on Thekla's face as she gathered the Tattletales around her on the playground last Thursday. A look of cunning. He knew that look. He admired it and feared it. She was a schemer, and she was after him. No doubt about it.

He almost fainted with terror at the notion, and he had to grab at a bough to keep from crashing headfirst to the ground. If Thekla Mustard had a secret crush on him, he'd have to persuade his dad to quit his job and his mom to sell the house. They'd have to move, someplace very far away. Wyoming. Nevada. Alaska. The moon. How could anyone ever be safe from the love of Thekla Mustard?

He couldn't tell the boys about it—not yet. He'd keep his lonely terror to himself. But he'd better keep on his guard, too. If Thekla stopped sticking her tongue out at him and blew him even one single kiss across the classroom instead, his reputation would be ruined. He'd have to resign in disgrace from his position as Chief of the Copycats Club.

Fawn put the cupids' nest on the floor in her closet. She left the closet door open so that the heat from the radiator would seep in. Fawn was proud of the nest. She had shredded a couple of the haunted hairdo wigs with which the Tattletales had scared the Copycats last November. She fluffed up the hair in a cardboard carton so that the cupids could burrow in it like hamsters in straw. Then she supplied them with a whole jar of peanut butter.

"Yum, yum," said Milos, trying peanut butter on the end of a crayon. "Peanut butter's good, but red crayons are better."

"Yesterday I kept hearing the most boring song," said Rhoda. "More of your terrible soulless music. Over and over, a chime like someone just learning to play."

Fawn thought. "Oh, that's the telephone ringing," she said. "People calling to, like, make beauty appointments, or cancel them."

"People call like that? People in Vermont have funny voices. They should hear a naiad sing her stream melodies, and learn a little something about music."

Fawn couldn't explain how a telephone worked so she just said nothing.

On Monday, Fawn said, "Now we must go back to school to do our work. Miss Earth and Chad Hunkley: love at first sight. It's cold outside, but I'll try to hug my knapsack to keep you warm."

"Oh, more of your cold world," said Rhoda. "If we must, then we must. I hope we don't smash into any invisible ice walls again."

"Windows, windows," said Fawn. "They're called windows."

Fawn could hear the little cupid teeth chattering just during the quick run from the door of the Hamlet House of Beauty to School Bus Number 3. The other Tattletales on the bus fell silent when Fawn got on, because they knew the cupids were with her. However, the bus still throbbed with noise. Depending on whether or not they'd finished their weekend homework, thirty-seven other kids shrieked with happiness or terror. The normal Monday morning panic.

Sammy Grubb was worried about the note from the secret admirer. He was certain it had come from Thekla Mustard. It had to. He saw Thekla looking intent, focused, more like a dictator-on-training-wheels than ever. He'd better be on his sharpest alert for danger.

He sat on the school bus, willing his eyes to stare straight ahead at the ice-slicked road. He looked neither left nor right. He didn't want his glance to fall on Thekla even accidentally. "Hey, Sammy, what's wrong with you?" said Hector Yellow, sitting next to him.

"Got a stiff neck from the cold weather," said Sammy, not turning.

Across the aisle, Lois Kennedy the Third was wondering how she could talk the cupids into shooting a pair of arrows at Sammy Grubb and Thekla Mustard. Lois would have sat next to Fawn on the bus if she could, but Fawn usually sat with the third graders. Lois guessed that sitting with little kids made Fawn feel smart—at least smarter than them. It must be awful to feel stupid.

Lois thought: I sure enjoy being smart enough to have such a good nasty plan in my head.

Thekla Mustard was feeling mean and powerful. So she hadn't gotten any special secret admirer valentines. So *big deal.* Who needed mere greeting-card sentiment when you had an arsenal of the real McCoys at your disposal?

Superman's X-ray vision, Luke Skywalker's light saber, Peter Pan's magic flying sparkles? Hah! Piffle. Eight magic arrows poisoned with love dust were worth more than any other weapon you could name.

She caught sight of her reflection in the window and nodded grimly at herself. The execution of authority was a lonesome business. The very idea of the word *superior* meant "alone above the others." Alone. That was the price of power. Oh, well.

Pearl Hotchkiss walked to school, wondering if Sammy Grubb had found her secret admirer's valentine. Would he guess it was from her?

Once at school, Fawn stuffed her knapsack under the chair. "Ow," said a voice from within. "Rhoda, Naxos almost poked poor Milos in the eye."

Naxos said, "Well, Milos almost poked Naxos first. *A-B-C-D-E-F-G, no one's more annoyed than—*"

"If you boys don't settle down . . ." came Rhoda's voice threateningly.

"Shh," whispered Fawn. "We're doing well. Don't give yourselves away!"

"Class," said Miss Earth, looking up from her lesson plan. "A little too much noise here. Before the bell rings, it's Drop Everything and Read time. Who's doing all that morning mumbling? Does everyone have a book?"

Everybody mumbled, and then remembered they weren't supposed to mumble in the morning.

"Show me," said Miss Earth.

They lifted up a display of brightly colored paperbacks. Except for Fawn, who would rather look at picture books, Miss Earth's students loved to read. Miss Earth glanced at the array of fine titles. *Sarah Plain and Tall. The Twits. The Great Gilly Hopkins. The Lion, the Witch, and the Wardrobe.* Various Goosebumps, Volumes 26, 72, and 312. One of the Harry Potter books. *The Fledgling. Stone Fox. The Ear, the Eye, and the Arm. Encyclopedia Brown Bites the Dust.* American Girls Number 14. The Folger Library edition of Shakespeare's *A Midsummer Night's Dream.* (That was Thekla Mustard's book. She enjoyed reading about summer in the middle of winter.)

"Where's your book, Fawn?" said Miss Earth.

Fawn was rereading *Where the Wild Things Are,* because she liked the drawings. The monsters reminded her of people who came into the Hamlet House of Beauty for washes, rinses, and sets. "My book is in my knapsack, Miss Earth," said Fawn.

"Get it out," said Miss Earth. She didn't mind that Fawn liked picture books. Sometimes Miss Earth read picture books to the class. "Why should you stop reading picture books just because you can read chapter books?" she would say. "Do you stop eating doughnuts just because you develop a taste for pizza?"

Miss Earth finished looking over her lesson plans. She took a sip of her morning tea. Then she got out her own book to read for the last five minutes of Drop Everything and Read time. She was enjoying *Mauled in Manhattan.* The killer crocodiles had just swum across New York Harbor. They were chasing a bunch of tourists up the steps inside the Statue of Liberty, all the way to the torch. Only Spangles O'Leary, the heroine, could save the day. Miss Earth couldn't wait to find out how.

Because teachers see almost everything, out of the corner of her eye Miss Earth noticed Fawn lean over and unbuckle the latches of her knapsack. But she didn't think anything of it. She thought Fawn was getting out *Where the Wild Things Are*. In a way, that's exactly what Fawn was doing, if you consider a cupid on the job to be something of a wild thing.

Milos slipped out and looked around the room. He flexed his little muscles and pointed at himself. My turn, he meant. Brave me, huzzah and hurray.

Fawn made a sign: Wait a minute. Then she murmured, "Thekla. We're ready."

"No murmuring," murmured Miss Earth automatically, caught up in her book.

Thekla turned to the back of *A Midsummer Night's Dream*. She pulled out a square of paper. It was a page from *TV Guide*. A full-color picture of the Great Jaw of Morning TV himself, Chad Hunkley. He looked like one of those faces carved in rock on Mount Rushmore, only a little more rocklike.

Thekla tiptoed to the front of the room.

"What is it?" said Miss Earth in a soft voice.

"I forgot to throw out my gum before I came into class," said Thekla.

This was a lame excuse, because Thekla was too superior to chew gum. Miss Earth should have caught this. But the power of Stephanie Queen's prose held Miss

Earth in thrall. She merely nodded and murmured, "You know where the basket is."

From her mouth Thekla removed the decoy piece of gum. She stuck it to the back of the page from the *TV Guide*. Then, just behind Miss Earth's back, she pressed the glossy photo of Chad Hunkley to the blackboard. All the Tattletales were watching closely. Pearl Hotchkiss and the boys in the class began to look up from their books, realizing that something was going on. "I—don't—believe it—" hissed Sammy Grubb in a voice too low to carry to the front of the room.

Milos fluttered up to the top of Fawn's desk. Fawn sat just behind Nina Bueno. "Nina," whispered Fawn. "Move over. Milos needs a clear view."

"No whispering," whispered Miss Earth.

Nina obeyed Fawn. Milos took the two arrows from his quiver. His plump little hands shook with excitement. "Milos is a marvel!" he said.

"Milos is a moron," said Naxos from inside the knapsack.

Milos laid one arrow against his bowstring. He drew both the string and the arrow back. He was trembling from the cold, even though the school's radiators had begun their usual morning clanking.

"No clanking," complained Miss Earth automatically. The radiators stopped clanking.

Milos released the arrow. It zizzed with the sound of a Ziploc plastic bag being opened.

"No zizzing—*oww!*" said Miss Earth. She clapped her hand on her shoulder, and her book fell back against her desk. *"Ow-ow-ow."*

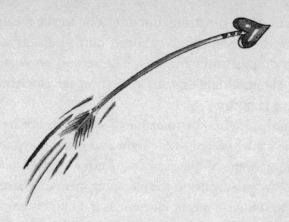

Milos had hit his mark! Miss Earth glanced around. The arrow had fallen behind her, and she didn't see it. "There can't be bees in the classroom in mid-February," she said. "Ooh, that smarts."

"No smarting," said Lois Kennedy the Third. She knew that was rude. But she wanted Miss Earth to look at her, so that Miss Earth wouldn't catch sight of Milos, who was fitting the second arrow to his bow.

"Lois, no smart-mouthing," said Miss Earth. "Understand?"

"Sorry," said Lois. "I'm reading Roald Dahl, and I think he's a bad influence."

"Don't lay the blame at someone else's door," said Miss Earth. "That's cowardly. Take responsibility for your own behavior, Lois."

Milos saw a pencil on Fawn's desk. He got a greedy look in his eye. He picked up the pencil, bit off the pink eraser, and chewed it as if it were taffy. "Energy," he whispered to Fawn. "To keep up my strength." Then he squinted and pulled the back the string. But just as he let the arrow fly, he burped—a somewhat rubbery burp—and his laurel wreath dropped over his eyes. The second arrow zizzed wildly about. It didn't go anywhere near the glossy photo of Chad Hunkley.

"I *do* hear a bee, or something," said Miss Earth.

The arrow veered to the right and came down in the terrarium, home of the class frog, Kermit the Hermit.

The frog never heard the incoming missile. The arrow zizzed as if it were meant for him, as if it had his name on it. It landed lightly onto the webbed skin between his front fingers, or toes, or whatever they were. The arrow punctured the skin, then fell over.

Kermit said, "Ribbet. Ribbet." He seemed surprised; usually he preferred to keep his comments to himself.

"Ribbet?" he said again, and jumped to the top of the plastic tower that Miss Earth had installed in the terrarium. "Ribbet?" he said.

"Kermit is speaking to me," said Miss Earth. "How friendly."

"Ribbet," said Kermit, as if agreeing. "Ribbet!" He gave a mighty hop and vaulted himself right out of the glass case. He landed on top of a stack of cardboard milk cartons that the class was collecting for a science project. He and Miss Earth locked eyes.

A silence swept through the room.

11

Kissing Kermit the Hermit

What an attractive frog," said Miss Earth. "I never noticed before."

"Ribbet," said Kermit. He blinked his eyes and looked back at Miss Earth.

Fawn was busy pushing Milos back into the knapsack with the other cupids. Luckily, Miss Earth was too distracted by Kermit to notice Fawn. "Kermit wants a little exercise," said Miss Earth. "How unusual. Kermit, come."

Kermit took a mighty hop and landed on Miss Earth's desk.

"I never noticed before how appealing frogs are," said Miss Earth. Then she shook her head as if to clear a fog from her brain. Or was she trying to clear a frog from her brain? "Still, we must do our work." She looked at her lesson plan. "Put away your books, children, and we'll start with word problems. We'll do the first few out loud. Is everyone ready to concentrate?"

No one was ready. Everyone was staring at Kermit and Miss Earth. A terrible truth was dawning on the boys as well as the girls. *The cupids as agents of doom.* Holy cow.

Miss Earth seemed not to notice the shocked stillness of her students. It was as if she was under a spell, or in a waking coma of some sort. Sleepwalking through her job. With unlikely blandness, she flipped over the pages of her teaching manual. "Now, take notes on what you hear," she said. "Then raise your hand if you can figure out the answer. Here's question number one." Miss Earth frowned at her book. "Maybe I could change this to make it more interesting. Everybody ready?" She smiled blazingly at Kermit, who didn't smile back only because frogs don't really smile.

"Heading east, a handsome frog is driving a car at forty miles an hour. One hundred miles away, an attractive young woman is driving her motorcycle due west at sixty miles an hour. If they both set out at two P.M., what time will they meet and fall in love?"

"Never!" cried Thekla. "Because the frog is going to hit a pothole and fly out the car window, and the woman is going to run over him with her motorcycle!"

"How cruel . . . and also incorrect," said Miss Earth. "Think before you speak."

"Never!" cried Sammy Grubb. "Because the story is unclear *where* they are starting from. Though they set out at the same time, the woman may live west of the frog, so she heads west, and the frog one hundred miles away is going east. Their paths won't cross. Better that way."

"Presume the woman lives east of the frog," said Miss Earth.

"I can make no such presumption," said Sammy starchily.

"Anyone here who can tell us?"

"Three P.M.," said Forest Eugene Mopp. "Though,

84

speaking as the resident Mr. Science, may I add that such a romance is unlikely, as well as unsavory to imagine."

"Good job," said Miss Earth. "Does everyone understand how Forest Eugene worked out the answer?" She explained it. No one was listening except Kermit, who had never shown any interest in math problems before.

Miss Earth put down her book. "I'll make up the next question," she said. "If a frog croaked out a love song from the bottom of a bog, and his true love knew that only one kiss could restore him to his real human self, what would he look like?" Miss Earth chewed on the nail of her little finger. "Oh, that doesn't sound much like a math problem, does it?"

"He would look like Chad Hunkley," said Thekla Mustard, "whose picture happens to be hanging behind your desk, Miss Earth. Take a look."

While Miss Earth swiveled in her chair to see, Fawn

Petros raced to the front of the room and snatched Kermit the Hermit from Miss Earth's desk. Then Fawn ran back to her desk and stuffed him in the knapsack with Milos and the other cupids.

"If you must know," said Miss Earth, "Chad Hunkley makes me want to blow up the TV with dynamite." She turned back. "Oh, my goodness, where's Kermit gone?"

"Back into his hidey-hole," said Sammy. He had no wish to protect the girls by helping them cover up their crimes, but he thought Miss Earth would be better off without a frog boyfriend. "Kermit got shy again, as usual."

"Oh, well," said Miss Earth. She sighed. "Perhaps we should move on. I don't seem to have a head for math this morning, and neither do you. Shall we continue our literature unit on fairy tales?" She went over to the reading rocker. "*Famous Tales from Northern Europe*. Oh, here's one. *The Frog Prince.*"

From Fawn's knapsack, Kermit began to croak loudly.

"No croaking," said Miss Earth automatically, before she could catch herself. Then she looked around. "Is that Kermit the Hermit? Why's he croaking?"

"He wants to hear the story," said Hector. "Read on."

Miss Earth obliged. It was a good story about a princess who kissed a frog and turned him into a handsome prince. "What a smart princess," said Miss Earth when she had finished. "When faced with a creature covered with pond scum, she knew how to see the beautiful soul within. Now, where's Kermit?"

She wandered over to the terrarium as if she did it every

day. "Oh, Kermit," said Miss Earth. ""It's time to leave your monastic life, Kermit, and rejoin the human race!"

The children watched her closely. Was it possible she was laying this on a little thick? Or could she really be so enchanted as to suffer a paralysis of her normal salt-of-the-earth personality?

Miss Earth shook the terrarium gently to make Kermit the Hermit come out of his hidey-hole. Just then there was an interruption. It was Principal Hetty Buttle on the intercom.

"Miss Earth?" said Principal Hetty Buttle.

Miss Earth snapped to attention. "Yes, Principal Buttle," she said.

"The kindergarten teacher has asked me if you could bring your class down early today, so they could do modeling clay with their kindergarten buddies before recess. Would you bring your students to the kindergarten—of course, reminding them not to run in the halls?"

"As you wish," said Miss Earth. "Roger, over and out."

Miss Earth shook her head. "What an odd day this is," she said. "Well, duty calls. We'll have to come back to Kermit the Hermit later. We're going down to our kindergarten buddies to help them with their modeling clay. Their teacher, Ms. Frazzle, will tell us what to do. Fawn, leave your knapsack here. Ms. Frazzle has all the supplies we need."

"But," said Fawn. "But—but—"

Miss Earth gave her a look. Fawn put her knapsack back under her desk. She hated to leave the cupids behind. What if hungry Milos tried to have a meal of frog's legs? Poor Kermit.

Miss Earth and her students walked soberly to the kindergarten class. Though Ms. Frazzle wasn't a first-year teacher, the kindergartners were first-year kindergartners. Her job was to calm them down. Their job was to rile her up. They seemed to be winning.

"Today," Ms. Frazzle said, with a wild look in her eye, "we're making snakes out of modeling clay. Miss Earth's students, do you remember who your little partners are? Bobby, stop biting Billy. Billy, don't slam your book on Kelly's finger. Krissy, get down from that window sill. Kevvy, hands off that fire extinguisher. Candy, your feet belong on the floor and your hands on the desk, not the other way around. Thank you. Sandy, if I have to tell you one more time to stop showing us your boo-boo . . . All right, who wants to help me pass out modeling clay?" Ms. Frazzle was lost in a mob of kindergartners.

"Why do we have to make snakes?" said Miss Earth to Ms. Frazzle.

"It's the only thing they can do so far," said Ms. Frazzle. "You know, roll out snakes, or ropes, or hot dogs, whatever you want to call them. We mustn't push them faster than they can go."

"Let's have them make frogs," said Miss Earth.

"It's snakes today," said Ms. Frazzle. "Says so in the lesson plan."

"I'd love to see some frogs," said Miss Earth.

"Then move to a swamp," said Ms. Frazzle. She wasn't having a good day.

At the little kindergarten tables, Miss Earth's kids knelt down to help their buddies make snakes. "Mine is a piece of spaghetti," said one tot. "Mine is a shoelace," said another. "Mine is a fiberoptic thread," said a third, "and you can use it in brain surgery."

"Good grief, I need my head examined," said Ms. Frazzle, almost to herself. "Why, oh why, oh why didn't I go into stunt parachute work when I had the chance?"

The kindergartners finished making their snakes in about a minute. "It's so hard to keep up with them," said Ms. Frazzle. "What next? Calculus? The rise and fall of the Roman Empire? The development of double-entry bookkeeping in twelfth-century Florence? Why don't they teach you anything *useful* in teacher education classes, like how to survive?"

"I'm going to go back and find Kermit the Hermit," said Miss Earth. "Perhaps if the children see a real live frog, they'll know how to make one out of clay."

The kindergartners were braiding their snakes together to make a wreath of snakes. "It's a hat for Ms. Frazzle!" someone said. "Let's put it on her!" They cornered their poor teacher behind her desk.

"Miss Earth!" cried Fawn, worried that Miss Earth would hear the frog croaking and then discover the cupids in Fawn's knapsack.

"Yes, Fawn?" said Miss Earth.

Fawn stood there thinking. She couldn't come up with a plan so fast. She felt sick with worry.

"Yes, Fawn, what is it?" said Miss Earth.

"I feel sick," Fawn said at last, which was true enough. "I have to go home."

Though she was under the spell of a cupid's sting,

Miss Earth was still first and foremost a teacher. She seemed to struggle to put thoughts of Kermit aside. She felt Fawn's forehead. "You seem normal to me, but let's not take any chances. I'll send you down to Nurse Crisp. She can take your temperature and call for your mother if need be."

"I'd better get my knapsack and coat first, in case I have to go straight home," said Fawn.

"All right," said Miss Earth. She began to lecture her students on good behavior so she could leave them for a moment to go find Kermit.

Fawn tore out of the kindergarten room and raced down the hall. From the other end of the school came a warning shout from Principal Hetty Buttle: "Someone is running in the corridor!" Fawn slowed down.

In the classroom, she snatched up her knapsack and her coat. On her way back to the nurse's office, she passed Miss Earth in the hall. Miss Earth looked like a stunned survivor of a roller coaster crash. She was humming "Froggie Went a-Courtin'." Kermit was still bouncing around in Fawn's knapsack with the cupids. He was signaling Miss Earth, ribbeting with unusual passion. Miss Earth didn't hear him, since she was singing to herself with her usual complete absence of melody.

"Shh," said Fawn. The frog settled down. There was no word from the cupids. Good. They'd really learned the necessity for silence.

At the health office, Nurse Pinky Crisp put a thermometer in Fawn's mouth. Then the nurse went to call Mrs. Petros to tell her Fawn wasn't feeling well. While

Nurse Crisp was out of the room, Fawn took the thermometer out of her mouth. Weren't the cupids always complaining of the cold? She'd stick the thermometer in Kos's mouth to cool it down, and then replace it in her own mouth just before Nurse Crisp came back. That would make Fawn seem sick and ensure her safe evacuation from school.

She opened her knapsack. The cupids had flown the coop.

"Oh, those stupid cupids!" said Fawn, despite herself. "Don't they know they'll get lost?"

She put the thermometer down and checked all the other little pockets of her knapsack in case she'd overlooked the cupids. But she hadn't. What to do, what to do, she said to herself. Think. *Think.* But telling herself to think only made her repeat the word in her mind (*thinkthinkthinkthink*), which was not only unhelpful but downright distracting.

Instead, she tried to picture where they might have gone. Once the class had cleared out, the cupids would have noticed the silence. They must have crept out of the knapsack. Fawn thought they finally had mastered the concept of windows, so she doubted they'd try to buzz their way through the glass, as dumb flies sometimes do.

No, the cupids couldn't get out. The doors were too heavy, and all the windows were closed in this weather. If the cupids couldn't get out, they'd choose to get warm.

The warmest place in the school was the furnace room downstairs.

Just then Nurse Crisp came through the door, carrying a stack of gauze bandages for the tending of wounds suffered on the battleground of the schoolyard. Fawn stuck the thermometer under her tongue before Nurse Crisp finished piling the cotton bandages on a shelf. Then Nurse Crisp removed the thermometer.

Nurse Crisp looked worried. "Mercy, that's a *low* temperature," she said. "Good thing your mother is driving over to get you. I'm sure you'll feel better once you get home. But make sure you have some chicken soup, and stay bundled up."

Fawn closed her eyes in relief. From down the long, echoey corridor, she could hear Miss Earth calling, "Kermit? Kermit the Hermit? Kermit, my friend? Where are you?" There was a sound of mild panic in her voice.

Nurse Crisp released Fawn with instructions that she should wait in the lobby by the front door. Fawn nodded. Once the corridor was free of passersby, however, she ducked down the basement steps.

The school janitor, Jasper Stripe, maintained his office and workspace in the furnace room. He always left the doors open so the heat of the boiler could help warm the school through the flow of air as well as through the hot water in the radiators. If Fawn could follow the roar of the furnace, so could the cupids.

With his back to the door, Jasper Stripe sat in an old lawn chair with crisscross nylon webbing. He was stationed in front of a portable television tuned in to *Court TV.* He was busy rewiring a school toaster in his lap while he watched. The cupids were all perched on a pipe running just below the joists of the floorboards overhead. They looked like four fat pigeons glued to their favorite show. Fawn gave them a stern look. She pointed to the mouth of the open knapsack. One by one they left the perch and fluttered into the knapsack. When they were all safely inside, Fawn tiptoed back up the stairs.

She couldn't help saying, "You ought to be ashamed of yourselves! I was sick with worry—do you hear me, sick!"

"Imagine how our mothers feel, after two thousand years," said Rhoda, rather belligerently. "By the way, was that stupid noisy flat face in the box the spirit of this place?"

Fawn didn't answer. Her mother was honking the horn outside the school. Fawn pushed through the door into the frigid February morning, knowing the cold air would shock the sensitive cupids into silence. It did.

12

The Sting of Naxos

Fawn's mother was worried about Fawn's low temperature. So she packed Fawn into bed and got her some weak tea and a hot-water bottle. Then she piled on two afghans and a tartan blanket. Finally Fawn said, "Stop, you're crushing me to death."

"I'll get you a book. What do you want?" said Mrs. Petros.

"Can I have that picture book about Antarctica?" said Fawn.

"You mean the nice big one Daddy sent?"

"No," said Fawn. "That has too many words. I want the one with the drawings and photos."

"Antarctica: Ya Gotta Love It," said Mrs. Petros. "Is it in your knapsack?" She picked up the knapsack and began to unbuckle it.

"Nooooo!" shouted Fawn.

Mrs. Petros gave her a look. "Temper, temper. I'd say at least your lungs seem healthy enough. Where is it, then?"

"I don't know."

Mrs. Petros was well equipped with the locating instincts of a mother. She found the book underneath the basket of clean laundry. "I've got a customer any minute, hon," she said to her daughter. "Will you be okay up here?"

Fawn tried to look sick enough to have deserved to come home, yet well enough to be able to be left on her own. She lolled her head on the pillow but nodded briskly at her mother. Mrs. Petros bought it. She left to give Sammy Grubb's mother an egg shampoo and to check up on the latest rumor that Mayor Grass was falling in love with Miss Earth. Taking part in local gossip was one of the rewards of being in hair management.

But as she rinsed her combs in sterilizing fluid, Mrs. Petros thought: Fawn's been acting strange lately. So secretive, in her room all the time, and that outbreak of temper. And now she's not feeling well. Maybe I should let her father know.

As soon as her mother had left, Fawn threw off the covers and grabbed her knapsack. Kermit the Hermit hopped out, looking for Miss Earth. He was followed by the cupids, tumbling in a roll of infant arms and fledgling wings.

"Why'd you zip away to the boiler room?" said Fawn.

"We did our job," said Rhoda frostily. "We shot our arrows. We wanted to go home. You left us alone, so we thought we'd find our own way."

"Greece isn't downstairs," said Fawn. "It's, like, far. But no one saw you fly downstairs, did they? Was everything cool? Are you all right?"

"We are fine. Treated like runaway piglets, but fine," said Rhoda. "Chilly, but fine. A little hungry maybe, but fine." She didn't sound fine. She sounded annoyed.

"Well, I'm glad *you're* so fine, because I'm not," said Fawn, throwing her head back on the pillow of her bed. "Our teacher has fallen in love with this, like, frog!"

"And the frog is having tender thoughts right back," said Rhoda, settling down on the headboard. But she seemed slightly ashamed. Smiling over-largely, she said, "At least one good thing comes from this. It proves we haven't lost our touch."

"You've lost your *aim*," Fawn pointed out. "Miss Earth can't be in love with Kermit the Hermit. For one thing, he's a *hermit*. For another, he's a *frog*! What are we going to do about it?"

"Poor Milos is sorry," said Milos.

"Milos is clumsy," said Naxos. "Shouldn't burp when aiming love arrows. Naxos never would." He strummed an arpeggio on his harp. *"A-B-C-D-E-F-G, no one aims as well as me."*

Kos, as usual, said nothing. He just took the peanut butter spoon and began to pound it on the floor, like a judge on *Court TV* pounding the gavel.

"When will the spell wear off?" said Fawn.

"It doesn't wear off," said Rhoda. "When will you take us home?"

"Not yet," said Fawn. "We have to do something first. 'Mr. Froggie Went a-Courtin' wasn't supposed to mean the frog courted a human *lady*! How do we rescue Miss Earth?"

Rhoda answered, "Well, if you insist, among us we cupids have three more pairs of arrows. If one of us helps Miss Earth fall *in* love with someone else, then she'll fall *out* of love with Kermit the Hermit. And once the spell is broken, he'll fall out of love with her, too."

"Don't worry, Fawn," said Naxos. He plucked a few more strings. "Naxos is a better aim than his clumsy burping twin brother."

Milos didn't answer. He was busy nibbling on the electric wire leading to the clown lamp. "The clown will electrocute you if you're not careful," said Fawn. "Stop that."

She went to find a new jar of peanut butter for the cupids, and a leaf of lettuce for the frog. When she came back, the cupids were looking at the pictures in the book on Antarctica. "Wow," said Rhoda. "This place is vast and cold. What is it, a book on Vermont?"

"No," said Fawn. "It's where my dad is. He studies penguins." She showed them a picture.

"Is that your dad?" said Rhoda.

"No, that's a penguin," Fawn told her.

"Why isn't your dad here?" said Rhoda.

Fawn told her. Science, work, money.

"But he loves you?" said Rhoda. "Surely he loves you."

"I think so." Fawn showed Rhoda the Valentine's card she had made for him. It was drawing of a heart with icicles dripping from it. "Keep warm," it said.

"You should say what you really feel," said Rhoda. "That's what love is about. What do you *really* feel?"

Fawn wanted her dad to come home. But what she said was, "A-B-C-D-E-F-G, when will Dad come home to me?"

"Then write that," said Rhoda. "Believe me. I know. This is my job. Say it, and send it. Promise? Fawn, do you promise?"

° ° °

The phone rang six times that evening. Mrs. Petros answered it and kept saying, "I'm sorry, honey, but Fawn is sick and can't come to the phone." It was the Tattletales calling, one by one, to find out what to do next.

The seventh time, Mrs. Petros heard a boy's voice. "Is that you, Sammy Grubb?" she said.

"Uh," said Sammy's voice, "ummm. Well, yes. It is. I'm—um—calling to see if Fawn needs her homework assignments. Since she went home sick."

Mrs. Petros could tell Sammy wasn't being truthful. But she guessed wrong. She thought that maybe Sammy *liked* Fawn. But really, Sammy was calling out of a mounting sense of horror. All the boys had seen what the cupid's arrows had done to Miss Earth. If those weapons ever fell into the wrong hands—Thekla's hands—well, it was almost too dreadful to contemplate. Thekla Mustard had already sent him a card. What if she commanded Fawn to deploy an arrow in his direction?

Not for nothing was Sammy Grubb the Chief of the Copycats. It was his job to face the gut-chilling truth, and hang the cost. "I need to talk to Fawn," he declared.

"She's resting. I'll tell her you called," said Mrs. Petros firmly. "Bye, Sammy." But she didn't keep her word. She didn't say anything to Fawn. Mrs. Petros thought love was a dangerous thing. And she also thought Fawn was too young to have a boyfriend yet.

Then Mrs. Petros placed a call herself, a very long-distance call. "Hello?" she said. "Dimitri? This is Gladys. I got your letter . . ."

On Tuesday morning Fawn said she felt better. She needed to get right back to school. Once again Fawn packed the cupids and Kermit in her knapsack—this time with a hot-water bottle to keep them all warm. But her mother insisted on driving her to school, so Fawn didn't get a chance to warn the Tattletales what was about to happen next.

When Mrs. Petros dropped Fawn off at the front door of the Josiah Fawcett Elementary School, the bells had already rung. The children were all in their classrooms. The principal, Hetty Buttle, was overseeing a crisis of spilled orange juice in the cafeteria. The school secretary, Mrs. Cobble, was helping the janitor lay down the athletic mats for gym. So Fawn ducked into the school office.

I'm a good girl, said Fawn to herself, but I have to be brave today. I promised Rhoda I would. I'll save up allowances for the rest of the month and leave money in an envelope that says: *To pay for the secret fax sent without permission.*

And then, her heart in her throat, Fawn inserted the Valentine's card for her dad in the school's fax machine. She dialed the numbers she'd copied down from her mom's address book. The machine perked up, *cherk-cherked* its codes, and the Valentine slipped through slowly. When it was released, Fawn grabbed it and dashed down the hall to Miss Earth's room, her knapsack bouncing on her back. Various remarks came through the pink nylon. "Ow!" "Ow!" "Boys, quiet now. Shh!" "Ribbet, ribbet."

Principal Hetty Buttle came out of the cafeteria. She raised a finger like a pistol and called, "Stop running in the halls, Miss Petros! Or you'll stay after school and wash the blackboards!"

Fawn slowed down. When she reached her classroom, she was surprised to see two figures standing in the front of the room. One was Miss Earth. The other was Cap'n Trueheart from the show called *Cap'n Trueheart*–not the actor who played him, but a big soft-edged pillowy Cap'n Trueheart, bouncing gently like a blow-up balloon, which he happened to be.

"Oh, Fawn, I'm glad you're feeling better," said Miss Earth. Her eyes looked bleary, as if she hadn't slept well. "I was just saying that after you left yesterday, I came back to our classroom to look for Kermit the Hermit. He seems to be lost. When Ms. Frazzle told the class to return, everyone came racing down the hall at top speed. Principal Buttle was not happy about the running in the halls. So she installed this life-size blow-up punching bag shaped like Cap'n Trueheart. She thought perhaps his Napoleonic uniform would have a sobering effect, like a school crossing guard's belt, or a police officer's badge. Since I think very little of that TV show I can't agree, but here he is anyway, to remind us not to run in the halls."

"But, Miss Earth," said Salim Bannerjee, "I still do not understand. It is natural for children to run and play."

"Yes, I know," said Miss Earth, "but Principal Buttle worries that children will slip on the melted snow tracked in from the playground. She wants to avoid having her students or teachers do themselves any harm. So the rule is: No running. And Cap'n Trueheart is here to remind us."

The children liked Principal Hetty Buttle. Some of them even watched that soppy *Cap'n Trueheart* show when they were lucky enough to stay home from school with raging fevers or pretend raging fevers. But it did seem a little peculiar for the principal to rely on a blow-up toy to keep order.

Fawn sat down. "What's that red heart on Cap'n Trueheart?" she said.

"Oh, that's a pincushion shaped like a heart," said Miss Earth. "I brought it from home to be a little pillow for Kermit the Hermit. But some anonymous romantic knave in this classroom taped it to Cap'n Trueheart instead. I haven't had a chance to take it off yet."

"It's a nice pincushion," said Pearl Hotchkiss, blushing. She was thinking she'd like to give it to Sammy Grubb, since he didn't seem to have noticed her secret admirer's Valentine's Day card.

"It was a present from Mayor Timothy Grass," said Miss Earth nonchalantly. "I don't like it much, frankly, but I thought Kermit might."

Thekla Mustard's ears perked up. Mayor Grass was giving little pincushion hearts as presents? Hmm.

Miss Earth still seemed to be in transports of affection for the frog. She said, "I worry about Kermit being missing. When Principal Buttle came down from the office yesterday afternoon to find out why I was still here, I had torn the room apart. I think maybe Principal Buttle felt sorry for me, and she was really loaning me her Cap'n Trueheart for company. For surely she can't think that a balloon would terrify students into sensible behavior. Sensible behavior comes from willpower that's inside you."

Was Miss Earth trying to talk herself into some sensible behavior of her own? Was she trying to seize hold of some willpower she'd misplaced? If so, she couldn't manage it. Romance was too powerful a spell. She was staring forlornly at the empty terrarium. Miss Earth glanced at Cap'n Trueheart as if to see whether he agreed. Thekla took this opportunity to swivel around and whisper to Fawn, "Are the cupids here? Now, Fawn, now! Try again!"

Fawn ripped open the top of her knapsack. It was Naxos's turn. He was ready with his two arrows. He fluttered out, the other three cupids just behind him. He steadied himself on the edge of Fawn's desk. "Psst, Nina, shove over!" hissed Fawn.

Thekla sneaked behind Miss Earth and taped up the picture of Chad Hunkley on the blackboard again. "What's that? Chad Hunkley, that fellow from the morning TV show?" said Miss Earth, frowning. Thekla skulked away, bumping into the Cap'n Trueheart balloon as she passed it.

"Ow! Bees again?" Miss Earth slapped her neck.

Milos rippled his fingers over Naxos's harp while Naxos swung the second arrow to his bow. "Kiss that froggie good-bye," muttered Naxos. He did a little dance and sang softly, *"A-B-C-D-E-F-G, 'Froggie Went a-Courtin' is history!"* He let the second arrow fly. It spun through the air like a paper wrapper blown off a straw: straight, true, and . . .

Whoops.

The Cap'n Trueheart balloon bobbed in front of Chad Hunkley's picture. Naxos's second arrow punctured the pincushion heart taped to Cap'n Trueheart's neck. Maybe the very tip of the arrow grazed the outer skin of the balloon, too. The balloon swayed back and forth, and Cap'n Trueheart's dizzy expression seemed even more abstracted than usual.

Kermit the Hermit hopped out of Fawn's knapsack, looking for his quiet terrarium. "Ribbet," he said, in a normal tone of croak.

"Oh, there's that pesky frog again. Somebody pick him up and put him away," said Miss Earth in a dazed voice. "Has everyone noticed how lifelike this balloon is?" She looked the rubber fellow in the eye. "You children know I don't think much of TV shows, but look, he's so—so *cute*."

13

Cap'n Trueheart

This is a genuine disaster," said Thekla Mustard. "Fawn Petros, can't you control those little nitwits of yours? Miss Earth is never going to fall in love with Chad Hunkley at this rate!"

Thekla wasn't even bothering to lower her voice. She didn't need to. Miss Earth was light-years away. She was humming the *Cap'n Trueheart* theme music. When played at the beginning of the show, the melody sounded like an orchestra of ninety-nine violins. When hummed by Miss Earth, the melody sounded like a bee trapped in her nose.

"Falling in love with a man is better than falling in love with a frog," said Naxos.

"But he's a *balloon!*" whispered Fawn.

Rhoda struggled out of the knapsack. She took one look at Miss Earth. Then she looked at the balloon. "Oh, woe," she said. "This is not good news, Naxos. We're never going to get home."

Miss Earth began playfully to punch Cap'n Trueheart. The harder she punched him away, the closer he came to her when he sprang back.

"This is awful!" hissed Sammy Grubb to Fawn Petros. "Why didn't you call me? Are you bonkers? How could you let them do such a stupid thing?"

"Call you? Why? And it wasn't stupid," said Fawn. "It was an accident."

"Look!" hissed Sammy. "Miss Earth is in love with a balloon! If that isn't stupid, I don't know what stupid is!"

"You *don't* know what stupid is," said Fawn, but saw that she was getting herself into a corner because the only thing she could say next was, *I'm* the stupid one. But she knew better than to say that aloud in front of her classmates.

Miss Earth remarked to the class, "Well, I'm sure Cap'n Trueheart will keep us all from running in the halls. We'd rather be in his buoyant company anyway. Maybe we'll stay in for recess."

"Noooooooo!" chorused all the kids.

"We'll see," said Miss Earth. She clasped her hands together as if trying to govern unfamiliar urges. Her eyes squeezed tightly closed. But the spell was too powerful. Even a strong personality like Miss Earth couldn't resist the pull of love. She opened her eyes and said in tender tones, "Perhaps we should have a creative writing session now. We can do stories on the theme of 'Falling in Love with a Stranger.' I'll give you a starter phrase. *When I woke up that strange morning, little did I know that by evening my heart would be . . .*"

Though they'd had no chance to agree on a single strategy, every student of Miss Earth's was filled with the same impulse: to take her mind off romance. They leaped

to the assignment like veteran warriors. "Little did I know that by evening my heart would be broken into bits," said Thekla Mustard harshly.

". . . eaten by raccoons," said Sammy Grubb.

". . . transplanted into the chest of a wild poodle," said Mike Saint Michael.

". . . trampled by gypsy dancers," said Sharday Wren, doing a little twirl.

". . . frying in a little olive oil and crushed garlic," said Anna Maria Mastrangelo.

". . . pulsing under a neutron microscope at NASA headquarters," said Forest Eugene Mopp.

". . . hidden in a big bass drum at a concert," said Carly Garfunkel.

". . . packed in ice in a beer cooler," said Stan Tomaski.

". . . melting in a microwave oven like a marshmallow," said Nina Bueno.

". . . traumatized by a severe myocardial infarction," said Moshe Cohn, whose father was a doctor.

". . . hacked into pieces by a dull-bladed Cuisinart," said Lois Kennedy the Third.

". . . nailed to the door of the Castle of Doom," said Hector Yellow.

". . . pounded with a pestle to make curried Heart of Darkness," said Salim Bannerjee.

". . . struck by a stupid cupid's arrow," whispered Fawn Petros.

". . . so beset by heartburn that my students would have to *meet at recess for an emergency strategy session to plan my recovery!*" said Pearl Hotchkiss, signaling her fellow students. She continued irritably, "Miss Earth, this is the dumbest starter sentence you've ever given us!"

"There's no sentence so dull," said Miss Earth, "that a little imagination can't make it better. The same goes with life. Get to work, my sweets. I'll do one myself, as I always do." But as the children labored over their stories, Miss Earth could only stare into the unblinking expression of Cap'n Trueheart.

Most of the children finished their paragraphs and went on to do some reading. Only Fawn labored on. She wasn't very good at stories, but she tried.

Finally Miss Earth stirred herself to say, "Well, I suppose we should hear some of these stories. Fawn, would you like to start?"

"No, thank you," said Fawn. But Miss Earth gave her

a little look. So Fawn stood up and took a deep breath. The words seemed to swim before her eyes.

"Falling in Love with a Stranger," said Fawn Petros. "By Fawn Anastasia Petros."

"Very good so far," said Miss Earth. Then she turned to the balloon and said, "Cap'n Trueheart, listen through those beautiful painted ears of yours."

"Little did I know when I woke up that morning that by nighttime my heart would be struck by a stupid cupid's arrow," read Fawn. Most of that sentence she had copied off the blackboard, so it was easy to read.

"Nice beginning," said Miss Earth. "Go on."

"Well," said Fawn, "there's not much more, but I drew a picture." It was a figure of someone who looked like Miss Earth staring goonily at something that looked like Cap'n Trueheart.

The class clapped politely. They all got the idea.

"A bit skimpy," said Miss Earth. "Can you write some more?"

Luckily the recess bell rang. Miss Earth seemed to have forgotten her idea that her class should stay in for recess. To Fawn, it looked as if Miss Earth was wondering if she should share her glazed doughnut with her glazed boyfriend.

In the schoolyard, Mrs. Brill the lunch lady tramped about in the snow like a friendly ogre, keeping children from hurting each other by accident or on purpose. The Copycats, the Tattletales, and Pearl Hotchkiss met on a snowbank near the Dumpster. Fawn had her knapsack on her back. She didn't dare risk leaving the cupids alone in case they tried to fly away again. It was for their own good.

Sammy Grubb eyed Thekla Mustard warily. Oooh, what a cool character she was. She showed no sign of having sent him a secret valentine. The hardhearted Empress of the Tattletales was a brilliant actress. She was busy counting heads and looking perky and businesslike. "Fellow sympathizers," began Thekla, "there is trouble abroad."

Sammy Grubb wasn't going to be outdone. "Look here," he said, "lose the sound bites, Thekla. Talk real. First things first. Let's get rid of this Cap'n Trueheart balloon. We can't have Miss Earth in love with a rubberized sea captain. It'll get around town. She'll be a laughingstock."

"What is a laughingstock, anyway?" asked Fawn.

They all looked at her. Nobody actually knew.

"Is it like a laughing stocking?" said Fawn.

"Fawn," said Thekla kindly, "get a life."

"I have a life," said Fawn, more bravely than usual. "This *is* my life. That's the problem, Thekla!" She had a terrible feeling she was going to start to cry. Miss Earth had turned into a zombie of love, and it was all Fawn's fault.

"Well," said Thekla, who, though bossy, was not unkind. "Then learn from your life, Fawn, and tell us what we should do!"

"I don't know," said Fawn. "I wish that stupid balloon would just blow away!"

"It's not that kind of balloon," said Thekla. "It's filled with normal air, not helium."

But Sammy Grubb said, "Fawn, you're a genius! Over

at the general store they have a canister of helium! I made four bucks on Valentine's Day helping Bucky Clumpett fill up heart balloons made out of Mylar. I bet there's still some helium left! We could spirit Cap'n Trueheart over there before the lunch bell rings."

"We'd have to distract Miss Earth," said Thekla Mustard.

"You Tattletales better do that," said Sammy Grubb. "We Copycats will take care of giving Cap'n Trueheart a little lift."

"How about me?" said Pearl Hotchkiss. "I'm not a Copycat or a Tattletale. But I can still be useful."

"Can you keep the lunch lady busy?" said Sammy. "Mrs. Brill has an eagle eye. She wouldn't miss seven boys making a beeline across the green to the Clumpett's General Store. She'll think we are going there for candy."

"I'll do my best," said Pearl. Sammy grinned at her. She felt great.

The campaign swung into action. First the Tattletales rushed into the classroom. The girls moaned in pain. They pretended to have caught seven cases of frostbite in their fingers. Miss Earth was so busy helping the girls strip off their mittens and gloves that she didn't see the boys hustling Cap'n Trueheart out the door. "Odd, your fingers look pink and healthy, and feel warm enough," said Miss Earth to her girls.

Pearl Hotchkiss ran up to Mrs. Brill on the playground. "Mrs. Brill," she said, "do you know that today seven girls under your care have come down with finger frostbite so serious that they may never play jacks again?"

"What are you yapping about, Pearl?" cried Mrs. Brill heartily. "It's balmy today, a whole four degrees above zero!"

"Better safe than sorry," said Pearl. "Don't you think you should take the other kids inside till Nurse Crisp gets a chance to look at them?" Mrs. Brill did think so. She raised a commotion of whistles and instructions.

In the confusion, the boys dragged Cap'n Trueheart down the road and across the snowy green. Bucky Clumpett was out in the back room of the general store, supervising a delivery of sad-looking midwinter produce. With nervous fingers, the boys removed the cap from the balloon's air plug. Then they all jumped up and down on Cap'n Trueheart to force the air out of him. He ended up looking like a deflated rubber raft. His flat face stared up from the floor at them all, as if to say, "Go ahead, walk all over me. That's what love will do to you."

Then Sammy attached the hose of the helium canister to Cap'n Trueheart and opened the valve. There was a little hiss. Cap'n Trueheart began to look more interested in life again.

When they came out of Clumpett's General Store, the schoolyard was empty. "Pearl did a good job making sure the coast was clear," said Salim. "We've still got five minutes left to lunch period."

"Hold this guy down," said Sammy. "We don't want to lose him before we're ready."

The seven Copycats held Cap'n Trueheart under their arms like Visigoths handling a battering ram. They rushed him up the road and into the Josiah Fawcett Elementary

School. Luckily, the halls were clear. They ran down the hall with Cap'n Trueheart.

"No running in the halls!" yelled Principal Buttle. The boys slowed to a pace that was part gallop, part stroll. They pushed into Miss Earth's classroom. Their teacher didn't see them. She was on her knees, bending over Carly Garfunkel, who had pretended to faint from frostbite. The boys whisked Cap'n Trueheart over to the side of the desk he had stood on before. Then they opened the door that led out into the schoolyard.

Miss Earth turned. "Close that door!" she exclaimed. "There are dangerous bouts of frostbite going around! Though I've lived in Vermont my whole life, I've never seen the likes . . ."

Sammy Grubb gave Cap'n Trueheart a little nudge. The rubberized sea captain bounced a little, and headed for the door.

Miss Earth hurried after the gently bobbing Cap'n Trueheart, who was inching along in the draft. She was able to catch hold of the red heart-shaped pincushion that someone had taped to his chest. The pincushion came off in her hands. Now the balloon had nothing to weigh it down. It went headfirst out the door, and began to turn slow cartwheels as it lifted away from the school.

Miss Earth ran into the schoolyard. Principal Buttle was close behind her. "Come back!" cried Miss Earth. "Come back!"

"I say," said Principal Buttle. "The ones who want to be like that? Let 'em go. Good riddance to flighty men."

In the classroom, Fawn was scolding the cupids. "This is turning into a disaster!"

"It's always serious when lovers fly away," said Rhoda. But she sounded distracted. She was leaning over little Kos, who seemed to be shivering as if with a case of frostbite that wasn't fake. She looked up. "When are you going to take us on the school bus to Greece?"

Fawn had nothing to say. Rhoda still didn't get it, did she?

The babysitter cupid looked from face to face. "Where *is* Greece?" she asked again. "Where have you put it?" She pointed out the window toward Hardscrabble Hill. "Is it over there?" She turned and pointed in the direction of the Grand Union. "Is it that way?"

Thekla Mustard said, "Rhoda. Listen to me. Greece is a *very* far distance."

"But how far is very far?" said Rhoda, almost in tears.

"Do you know what *distance* means?" said Thekla.

Rhoda pretended to shoot an arrow, and trace its flight path in the air with her fingertip. "Distance is the space between people," she said.

"More than that," said Sammy. "It's also the space between places. Distance can be very far. *Very far* means 'quite a lot of far.'"

"I'm just stupid. I don't understand," said Rhoda. Her wings began to droop. "We need to go home. Kos is feeling the cold. There is too much distance between here and the warmth of Greece, wherever it is."

14

The Several Stings of Rhoda

The afternoon was worse than the morning. Miss Earth sniffled into her hankie so often that it began to look like a crumpled white carnation drowned in a flash flood. Fawn thought, The love created by these cupids' arrows is a doozy of a magic spell. How strong it seems! Is it as real as the love that ignites naturally between two people? Or is it realer?

Nurse Crisp came back in to the check the fingers. She took a dim view of Miss Earth's tears. She boomed, "Buck up, gal! There's work to be done. Why has this flash frostbite scare shivered your timbers? Get a hold of yourself."

"I'm sorry," said Miss Earth. "Class, continue with your social studies project. I'll be around to check your work in a moment." But moment after moment passed, and all she could do was tremble at her desk and hum the *Cap'n Trueheart* theme music.

Her students were too shocked at her reaction to the departure of Cap'n Trueheart to do anything but obey. They labored over their social studies projects. They had to select a country on a map and research it: who lived there, what the major tourist attraction was, exports, wildlife, and so on. (Fawn Petros had chosen Antarctica, and the answer to all of the questions was the same: penguins.)

Finally Principal Buttle came to the door. "Valentine's Day is the undoing of many a stalwart heart," she admitted. "Go home now and have a good cry, Germaine. Drink some tea. Watch something dumb and painless on the TV. I hear that *Cap'n Trueheart* is pretty reliable entertainment . . ."

As she wriggled into her coat, Miss Earth bawled so loudly that, from half the school away, even the kindergartners in Ms. Frazzle's class could hear her.

Principal Buttle took Miss Earth's place at the front of the room, but she wasn't used to teaching anymore. She perched on the edge of Miss Earth's desk for a few moments and said to the kids, "I can count on you all to behave yourselves, can't I?" Then she returned to the safety of her office.

As soon as they were alone, the children came right to the point. Naturally both Sammy Grubb and Thekla Mustard leaped to the front of the classroom. There was a disagreement about whether the Empress of the Tattletales or the Chief of the Copycats should chair the discussion. Pearl Hotchkiss spoke up. "I nominate myself, since I am the only kid in this room not affiliated with a club."

Fawn Petros surprised everyone by saying, "I second the nomination."

"All in favor," said Pearl, "say aye."

Twelve voices besides Pearl's said aye. Thekla voted for herself. Sammy voted for himself. "Me, by a landslide," said Pearl crisply. She settled down her fellow classmates. "Things are going from bad to worse here," she said. "For one thing, we've got to get those cupids home. For another, instead of making Miss Earth's life better, we seem to be making it worse. Should we just cancel this whole project right now?"

"And what?" snorted Thekla. "Leave her infatuated with a helium balloon that floated away? *Bad* idea."

"I agree," said Sammy. "This is seriously unhappy stuff."

"A few months ago," said Salim, "didn't Miss Earth herself tell us that only love can heal a haunting?"

"The only antidote to love," agreed Rhoda, poking her head out of the knapsack, "is more love."

"I don't know," said Thekla. "I've heard that chocolate bonbons are a good antidote to love. Also reruns of the *Dick Van Dyke Show* on Nick at Night. But let's be real. We have two secret weapons left—the arrows of Rhoda and Kos."

"But Naxos and Milos are good archers," said Rhoda. "I am out of practice. And, anyway, are you sure you have chosen the right love match for your teacher? A piece of paper with a bodyless head flattened on it? I know you call us stupid cupids, and maybe we are a bit dense, but—"

Thekla interrupted Rhoda and said, "Don't tell us our business. We make the rules. Besides, you could *practice*."

"If I practiced with my arrows, I'd use them up," said Rhoda.

Fawn said hesitatingly, "Maybe you could, like, practice with some pencils, maybe, or, like, some paintbrushes?"

Her classmates dropped their jaws. "Hey, Fawn," said Sammy cheerfully, "you had an idea!"

116

"A *good* idea," said Thekla with a condescending smile. "Your years as a member of the Tattletales are starting to pay off!"

"Practice makes perfect!" cried Pearl. "Everyone, to your desks! Find every stubby pencil, every leaky pen with the plug chewed off it, every paint-smeared water-color brush, every felt-tip marker! We'll help Rhoda train to be a champion! Round the clock! When Miss Earth comes in tomorrow morning, Rhoda will be the best trained archer of love in the Western Hemisphere!"

Rhoda said, "A little practice is not a bad idea. We don't have much more time to waste."

They set to work. It was amazing to watch. Once they set their minds to something, nothing could deflect them from it. Not even common sense.

But while the kids were hunting for practice arrows, Rhoda said to Fawn, "Did you send your message to your father, as I told you to? If you did, sooner or later happy days will return. Your problems will be solved. But I'm still troubled. I need to get these boys back to their moth-er. I have kept them out late—apparently twenty-three hundred years late. I'm ready to take these boys back to their home on Mount Olympus. I'm ready to treat myself to a little baklava. Maybe some pears in honey. Have you thought about how we are going to get back across that distance that is so hard to define?"

Fawn had to ask the crucial question that had been bothering her. "Will their mother still be there? Will yours? After all this time?"

"Why not?" said Rhoda. "It's true that time is a kind

of distance, too. But immortals are immortal. It means they don't die. Mount Olympus is a neat place to live because of that."

"Nobody is going to Mount Olympus," said Sharday, coming over. "Not till Miss Earth recovers from her Trueheart attack."

"Why don't you fly there on your wings?" said Nina.

"We're just kids," said Rhoda. "We would get tired flying as far as *far* seems to be. We'd fall. We'd get lost. Besides, this cold weather slows us down. I'm not sure we are able to fly as high as that Cap'n Trueheart balloon."

"We should have held on to him," said Anna Maria. "You could have ridden him home."

"He might be being hard to steer," said Rhoda. "Men usually are. I'd rather travel in our jug. The one we came in."

"But it's broken," said Fawn.

"Can't you find the pieces and mend it?" said Rhoda.

The girls looked at one another. Jasper Stripe the janitor emptied the trash every day, and once a week it was taken away by a dump truck. But the truck hadn't arrived yet. The shards of Greek pottery were probably still in the bottom of the big Dumpster out back.

"We'd like to help. But climb into a week's worth of kid trash and old lunches and pencil shavings and such? In the freezing cold?" said Thekla Mustard, flicking a loose thread off the starched lace of her collar. "Who would be so mad as to volunteer for that?"

"I will! I will!" cried Hector, Stan, Salim, Forest Eugene, Mike, and Moshe, overhearing. Sammy Grubb nodded without comment, accepting the task on behalf of the Copycats.

The boys went to rummage through the Dumpster. Jasper Stripe the janitor heard them. He came running from his room in the basement, his pipe hanging from his lips. "What the dickens are you doing in there?" he yelled. "Get outa there before the Board of Health closes us down!"

They told him what they were looking for. "I'll do any burrowing around here that's needed," said Jasper Stripe. "This is my turf. If I find what you want, I'll bring it to you tomorrow."

This had to do.

Meanwhile, the girls supervised Rhoda's archery practice. They sharpened pencils to serve as substitute arrows. Rhoda was older than the twins, of course, and her aim seemed to be better. But her problem was speed. She spent too much time fitting the pencil to the string. "Hurry," said Thekla. "Pick up the pace, Rhoda."

"I'm cold," said Rhoda. "Don't rush me."

"I *am* rushing you," snapped Thekla. "This is important. You gotta be able to see and respond at a moment's notice. Do you think we want a lunatic for a teacher? Hop to it, girl!"

"I'm doing my best," said Rhoda wearily.

"Do better than your best." Thekla sounded as if she had seen one too many inspirational movies about young ballerinas or karate kids or violin prodigies or Jedi

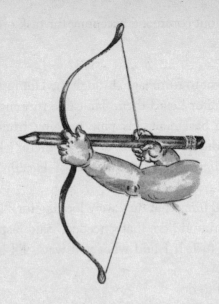

knights-in-training. "Do better than your best, Rhoda! Go the mile and beyond! Give it one hundred and ten percent! I want to see you come through with the whole enchilada!"

Rhoda whipped a pencil out of her quiver, whirled on her heel, pulled back the string, and let fly. The pencil hit Thekla right on the tip of her sternly wagging finger. "Ow!" said Thekla, examining the skin. "If I get lead poisoning, I'm suing you. Still, that was pretty fast, Rhoda. But I bet you can be faster yet."

At that moment the door opened. Sammy Grubb led the Copycats into the classroom. "Not good news, but not bad news," he managed to say before he was hit in the neck by a whizzing pencil, straight and true off Rhoda's bow.

"Is *that* fast enough for you?" said Rhoda to Thekla. "Queen of Impatience?"

"Hey, was that pencil loaded? I mean with love potion?" said Sammy worriedly, rubbing his neck.

"Figure it out for yourself," said Rhoda. "Everyone is so *bossy* here." She dived back into Fawn's knapsack and pulled the flap closed behind her.

The silence that followed made everything seem brittle and dangerous.

Lois Kennedy the Third began to smile. "Sammy Grubb," she said in a dangerously calm voice. "Rhoda had just sent a practice arrow-pencil right into the fingertip of Thekla Mustard. If your pencil was loaded, and hers was, too . . ."

"Don't be stupid," said Pearl Hotchkiss. What if Sammy fell in love with Thekla? How crushing. "Pencils aren't magic arrows."

"But they were shot by a cupid from a magic cupid's bow," said Lois. "Can't deny that, Pearl. Maybe the charm takes a little longer to work. Sammy and Thekla, *in love*. How do you feel, you two?"

Sammy was still. Thekla was trembling. They both stared at their feet. Thekla blushed a hot crimson. Sammy blanched a cool eggshell white. Then he shuffled his feet, and it was his turn to blush. Thekla looked up at the ceiling and sighed dramatically.

"Shall we leave you two little lovebirds alone?" said Lois coyly. "Perhaps the rest of the Copycats and the Tattletales should each meet and elect new leaders, since our former Empress and Chief clearly have no time for us anymore. I nominate myself as Interim Empress until such time as the matter can be decided."

Fawn was trying to hiss through the stitching of her knapsack. "Rhoda! Did you magic them into romance? Tell us!"

"Don't talk to me," said Rhoda. "Go away."

Pearl Hotchkiss said, "Oh, Sammy, don't throw your life away on *Thekla*!"

Thekla pressed her palms together as if in prayer, or perhaps she was about to burst into song. She blinked her eyes three times slowly and took a step toward Sammy Grubb.

The Tattletales fell back. The Copycats cowered as Sammy Grubb stuck his hands in his pockets, cleared his throat, and moved a step closer to Thekla.

"Somebody sent me a secret admirer's valentine," he said in a husky voice. "And I think I know who it had to be."

"Oh, do you now?" said Thekla in a high, rushed voice.

"I do," said Sammy. "I do, I do."

"I do, too," said Thekla. "Sammy, it—it—" She swallowed hard. "Sammy, it wasn't me."

"I know that," said Sammy sweetly.

"Because," said Thekla softly, forgivingly, "I'm trying not to be shy about saying this, so here goes: I loathe you just as much as I ever did, Sammy Grubb."

"And I you," he replied. "Glad that some things are forever. Now, let's get back to work."

"Right," said Thekla in her usual, tough-as-nails, business-as-usual, blasting-cap voice. Both Sammy and Thekla turned and lifted their chins. Their eyes were cold, staring across the room at Lois Kennedy the Third, who was looking pale.

"*You* sent the card to Sammy Grubb, didn't you?" said Thekla. "Intending to disgrace me, and then take over as Empress?"

"I never did!" said Lois.

"Of course you wouldn't admit it," said Sammy. "Boy, am I relieved to figure out who really sent the secret valentine, and that it didn't mean anything."

"You're just plain stupid," said Lois. "I don't even like you, Sammy Grubb."

But the kids had often heard Miss Earth say that people sometimes criticized each other to disguise the truth of their affections. No one was fooled by Lois's protests—except, of course, Pearl, who found herself relieved that she hadn't been revealed as the author of the secret valentine.

On the way home from school that day, Fawn left the bus and walked across Tyburn Road. She heard Rhoda's voice come thinly through the nylon of the knapsack. Fawn made sure no customer was approaching or leaving the Hamlet House of Beauty. She peered into the knapsack. "What?"

Rhoda peeped out. "I just hoped we were in Greece," she said. "We've given you four of our eight arrows." Her little head revolved, taking in the landscape. "What's that?" she said to Fawn, pointing at the ice-bound brook beside the road.

"That's Tyburn Creek," said Fawn.

"I'm not that stupid," said Rhoda. "That's no creek."

"It is," said Fawn sadly. "This winter is so cold that even Tyburn Creek has frozen over. The very bottom of it might still be running. Do you want to see?"

"You'd kill the very naiads of the streams with cold," said Rhoda, almost hysterical, "and listen instead to the prattling flat faces on that thing you call a TV? Have you no shame?"

"I don't know if we have any shame," said Fawn, "but we have satellite dishes partly because winter is so dark and cold and long here."

"If I can't go home to my mother and my motherland," said Rhoda, "I'd rather die."

"Please," said Fawn. "Please. Just one more try. We have to save Miss Earth. She's *our* mother. In a way."

The next day Miss Earth was back in school. She was dressed all in black, except for the red pincushion heart she had pinned to her lapel. The rims of her eyes matched the color of the pincushion.

Though she was filled with grief, still being under a charm of love, Miss Earth clearly was struggling against the spell, and trying hard to be a good teacher. "Fawn," she said, "do you still have a cold? You look bleary-eyed and awful."

So do you, thought Fawn, but she merely shrugged. The reason Fawn looked bleary-eyed and awful was that she had stayed awake all night long, helping Rhoda practice and talking to her about home. The other cupids had fallen asleep in their nest, which Fawn had moved near the radiator once she'd heard her mother turn in for the night.

Miss Earth said in a thin, uninterested voice, "Now, class, let us get our homework out. We'll start with science today. Remember we're studying—um—frogs." She shuddered.

Kermit the Hermit watched without expression.

When Miss Earth was busy flipping through the pages of the teachers' edition of the science book, Thekla Mustard marched up to the pencil sharpener in the front of the room. Once more she carried the now-wrinkled photo of Chad Hunkley. This time she tacked it on the bulletin board. If the arrow struck the photo, it would stick in the cork of the bulletin board behind it. No sense worrying about it bouncing off the hard surface of the blackboard.

Fawn opened her knapsack. Rhoda crawled out. Her arms were shaking. She looked bleary-eyed and awful, too, come to think of it.

"Champion!" said Fawn, to give her courage. "Olympic star!"

"Sleep," Rhoda mumbled. "I am so tired."

"You can do it! Ready," said Fawn. "Aim."

Rhoda readied. She aimed. Miss Earth was bending to get a clean handkerchief from her purse.

"Fire!" whispered Fawn.

Zing! went the string of the bow. "Ouch," said Miss Earth. "Bees *again*? We need fumigating. I had better call the janitor."

"Janitor's here," said Jasper Stripe, coming in the door.

He had a paper bag that was rattling with broken pieces of pottery. "What do you want me for?"

"Ready," said Fawn. "Aim . . ."

"Whoops," said Rhoda. The arrow zoomed. "Sorry," she said. "My arm is shaky. Fourteen straight hours of target practice, and I have no control left. It's not my fault."

"Miss Earth," said Jasper Stripe in a new, tender voice. "How lovely you look in black, with a red heart pinned to your lapel."

"Why, thank you, Mr. Stripe," said Miss Earth. She dried her eyes and smiled at him. "And how lovely you look in paint-spattered blue jeans and a ripped corduroy shirt."

"Oh, no," said Fawn.

Rhoda's wings drooped. She looked ready to cry.

♥

15

The Janitor Prince

The janitor and the teacher were mesmerized by each other. They wouldn't have noticed if a stink bomb went off between them. The kids abandoned all sense of caution.

"How stupid could you be!" said Sammy Grubb to Rhoda.

"I am not stupid. I am tired!" said Rhoda.

"Well, you were stupid not to realize you were so tired!" said Sammy.

"Don't call her stupid!" yelled Fawn. "Stupid is a stupid thing to call someone!"

"Well, you should know," muttered Sammy. But then he caught himself. "I'm sorry, Fawn. I didn't mean that."

Fawn was upset. "No, nobody ever *means* what they say, do they?" she said. "Then why do they say it? You say to Thekla, 'I hate you!' and then you say you don't mean it. But why do you say it? Why do you call me stupid? What's the use of words if you don't mean them? I think *words* are stupid!"

"Fawn," said Sammy Grubb. Then he did the one thing that boys in grade school never ever do. He put his arm around Fawn's shoulder and gave her a little hug.

"Ooooo-oooooooo-oooooh," the entire class called out. "True love!"

"I'm sorry I said something mean," said Sammy Grubb. "Fawn is right. We should listen to her more often. You're not stupid, Fawn. And I'm no first-class brain, either. Sometimes we just think in different ways and come up with different conclusions."

Fawn nodded. With effort, Rhoda flew up to her shoulder and gave her a little kiss. "I am sorry, Fawn," she said. "I have made my own big mistake and shot the wrong lover. My arms are too tired, and so is my heart."

"What should we do next?" asked Fawn. But nobody else seemed to know. They had gone back to staring at Miss Earth and Jasper Stripe.

Miss Earth was perched on the edge of her desk, having a chat with the janitor. Once again she seemed like only a ditzy shadow of her true self. "You married, Jaspy?" she was asking.

"Trash comes first," answered Jasper, somewhat evasively.

"I always liked trash," said Miss Earth. "You can make good art out of objects found in the dump. Once I saw a desk someone had thrown away, and I painted it for my mother and gave it to her for her birthday. I just love trash. Really."

Jasper Stripe was gazing in Miss Earth's eyes as if he could see barges full of lovely garbage floating there.

"Rhoda," said Fawn, "what *are* we going to do?"

But by now Rhoda had burrowed in the knapsack again. She was whimpering. "It's not my fault! You kept me up all night practicing. I'm *exhausted*! And I'm tired of being the baby-sitter for thousands of years! I don't care what the distance is! Every distance has two ends, and I'm ready to leave this end and go to the other one, however long it takes. I want to go home."

"Rhoda," said Fawn, "do you think if Kos got his arrows ready . . . ?"

Rhoda didn't even answer. She was too upset.

It was Pearl who marched up to Jasper Stripe and said, "Excuse me, Mr. Stripe, what's in the bag?"

"Pieces of a broken jug or something," said the janitor. "For the boys."

"Well," said Pearl, "did you hear that the main boiler's busted a gasket? I think it's gushing hot water all over the place."

"Work first," said Jasper Stripe to Miss Earth. He handed the paper bag to Sammy Grubb, and then he bounded out of the room. Miss Earth shook her head as if waking from a dream and murmured, "What a fellow! Now, class, where were we?"

"The study of frogs," said Thekla Mustard.

"Oh, maybe we should take a break on frogs," said Miss Earth. "I'll tell you what. For our fairy tale unit I'll read you another story. I'm sure it'll feature a brave young soul, someone you hardly expect to be a hero . . ."

"I can see what's coming," muttered Sammy Grubb. "Someone like a janitor?"

"A Janitor Prince," said Miss Earth. "I wonder if there is a story with that title?" She got out a book of fairy tales and looked in the index. But the closest she could find was Cinderella, which had ashes and cinders and rotting pumpkins in it.

Miss Earth was almost at the end of the story when there was a knock on the door. "Come in," she said in a high voice.

The door swung open to reveal Mayor Grass. Miss Earth's face fell. "Oh," she said. "I hoped it was the Janitor Prince."

"The *who*?" asked Tim Grass.

Miss Earth blushed.

"Miss Earth," said Mayor Grass, "you're blushing. Are you that glad to see me?" He began to twist his ski cap in his hands.

"Oh, not at all," said Miss Earth hurriedly.

"I see," said Mayor Grass in a dull voice. He looked as if what he saw was painful, and it hurt.

"Class, say good morning to Mayor Grass." Miss Earth managed to speak with an echo of her usual dulcet professional tone

"Good *morn*-ing, *May*-or *Grass*," they singsonged. Rhoda poked her head up out of the knapsack and took a good look at Mayor Grass.

"Nurse Pinky Crisp tells me you had a flash frostbite panic," he said to Miss Earth. "A number of chilled fingers. I thought I should come by and check it out."

"How sensible you are, and how kind," said Miss Earth in a voice more like her own.

He took her hand in his. "And are you all right?" he said gently. He rubbed her ring finger softly. "Are you really all right, Germaine?"

She shuddered and closed her eyes for just a second. Then she opened them and said, "Yes, Tim. Yes, I am. Girls, line up to have your hands inspected by Mayor Grass."

Mayor Grass looked at all the girls' fingers. He said, "I guess we have one hundred percent total recovery here. Well, girls, don't forget to wear your mittens and gloves. You, too, Miss Earth," he added. "Take care of yourself."

He was just leaving when the door opened again. There was Jasper Stripe pushing a wheeled metal bucket, full of soapy water. A mop was poking out of it. "Hi, there, Tim," said Jasper Stripe. To Miss Earth, he continued, "False alarm in the boiler room. Thought I'd do a little extra cleanup while I could. Want to be in your good book."

"You're a prince!" said Miss Earth, and batted her eyes.

Mayor Grass turned pale. His jaw dropped. He saw Miss Earth and Jasper Stripe making eyes at each other across a crowded room—crowded with students, that is. Almost to himself, he murmured, "Am I too late? Have I lost my chance?"

Rhoda turned her head and said to Fawn, "Is it my imagination, or did Mayor Grass have a nice expression on his face when he looked at your teacher? Maybe *he* is in love with her."

♥
16

The Sting of Baby Kos

After school let out, the children met for an emergency meeting at Fawn's house. They trooped through the beauty salon to the door leading to the upstairs apartment. Widow Wendell, who had nipped in to have a little touch-up of Living Color, said to Mrs. Petros, "Well, I guess being thick as a plank doesn't hurt her ability to make friends, does it?"

Mrs. Petros was fed up with Widow Wendell's nasty remarks about her daughter. "She's not thick as a plank, Mabel. And she's always had plenty of friends."

"Well, friends are important," said Widow Wendell. "Important when you're young, and important when you're old. I should know. I'm setting my cap for Mayor Grass. I ran into him at Clumpett's General Store an hour ago. He looked upset. He finally accepted the dinner invitation I have been lobbing at him for months. So make me look gorgeous, Gladys! I have a feeling tonight's the big night!"

Mrs. Petros sighed and reached for the blue hair rinse. She began to apply it. "Close your eyes. This can sting."

"Do you think Fawn's problems in school are caused by her having an absent father?" said Widow Wendell with her eyes closed.

"Fawn learns in her own way and in her own time,"

133

said Mrs. Petros. "Miss Earth is very happy with her progress. And so am I." She wanted to add: And it's none of your business, anyway.

"Still, we all long for something," said Widow Wendell. "I long to march up the aisle to the arms of Mayor Grass. I suppose Fawn longs for her father. Maybe she longs to be a bit brighter, too. What do you long for, Gladys?"

Revenge, thought Mrs. Petros. She reached to her counter for some yellow hair dye. She mixed the yellow dye with the blue rinse. Yellow and blue make green. "I'll do something extra special for you today," said Mrs. Petros blandly, "but you'll have to keep your scalp covered until just before dinnertime, or it won't work." From a cabinet she pulled out an opaque black rubber haircap. Just the thing.

Widow Wendell would never have her hair done here again. But Mrs. Petros didn't care. As she lathered up the green suds on Widow Wendell's head, she sighed. It was true, Fawn wasn't a good student. Was it because she missed her father? Was it possible Mr. Petros might come home for a visit soon? Gladys's phone call to him recently—what would it lead to? Mrs. Petros hated to get Fawn's hopes up, since Mr. Petros often changed his plans at the last moment. Better that Fawn should be surprised than disappointed.

Well, when Widow Wendell got home, she was going to be both surprised *and* disappointed.

Upstairs, the Copycats, the Tattletales, Pearl Hotchkiss, and the four cupids were all listening. The conversation between Widow Wendell and Mrs. Petros had floated up through the register. The children had heard every word.

Fawn was embarrassed that the entire town seemed to think she was slow. But her classmates didn't pay attention to that because of what Rhoda was saying.

"Is that woman interested in Mayor Grass?" said Rhoda. "I have begun to wonder if Mayor Grass is the *real* true love for Miss Earth."

"Could you be right?" said Thekla. "Mayor Grass loves Miss Earth? But Widow Wendell is about to nab Mayor Grass for herself! We must stop her!"

The boys in the room looked doubtful—even Hector, who usually kept an open mind.

But Rhoda said, "I agree. Shooting our arrows at a picture of a man is not the same thing as shooting at a *real* man. Look how well your Miss Earth and Janitor Jasper Stripe are falling in love, even if it is accidental. So it seems you must get Mayor Tim Grass into the classroom tomorrow. We'll fix this problem once and for all."

Sammy Grubb said, "Is this really the way to go? Look at the pickle Miss Earth is already in."

"Why is Miss Earth's being in love with Jasper Stripe a pickle?" said Lois Kennedy the Third. "Can't a teacher love a janitor? Can't a cat look at a king?"

"It's not that," said Sammy Grubb. "It's just that there's no proof they ever noticed each other before. Is it a good match? Jasper Stripe hides out in his basement office and watches *Court TV*. Miss Earth hates TV. She's committed to higher things, like culture and doughnuts."

"Besides, Mayor Grass is interested in Miss Earth," said Thekla Mustard. "Didn't Rhoda just tell us she thought so? And *she* should know."

"And," offered Salim Bannerjee, "if I remember correctly, when Mayor Grass disappeared over the Christmas holidays, Miss Earth shed a tear or two for him. Is this proof of love, or not?"

They all decided—even Pearl—that it was.

"Okay," said Rhoda. "I will help Kos do some target practice tonight. But not all night. He is a small cupid, and he needs his rest. With luck, by tomorrow all these problems will be solved. And then you will help us get home? Please?"

"Of course we will," said Fawn, and her classmates nodded vigorously. So Mike Saint Michael went to the mayor's office, which was in the town garage. Mike invited Mayor Grass to give a talk on classroom safety at Miss Earth's request. Promptly at ten o'clock.

The next morning, Jasper Stripe found a number of reasons to hang around Miss Earth's room and make repairs. He repainted the tip of the flagstaff. He restrung the wire on the back of the framed picture of George Washington. He dusted the leaves of the geraniums. He kept glancing shyly at Miss Earth. She kept glancing shyly back at him.

The students rolled their eyes. So much shyness! Love could sure be a headache.

Where was Mayor Grass, though? Ten o'clock came, and he didn't show up. Miss Earth was about to take her students to visit their buddies in Ms. Frazzle's kindergarten class. If Mayor Grass arrived and found no one in the classroom, he might leave. Jasper Stripe might propose marriage to Miss Earth by lunchtime. She might accept by recess. They might elope by nightfall. By the time she took attendance tomorrow, she might be Mrs. Stripe!

It was time for serious action. They had to stall, to keep Miss Earth in the classroom until Mayor Grass arrived. Thekla leaped to her feet. "Miss Earth!" she said. "I checked over the videotape from the show-and-tell session last week. I found the segment on snowy owls. I can play it now if Jasper Stripe gets the video recorder."

Miss Earth smiled. "An excellent idea," she said. "Mr. Stripe, would you?"

"I'm at your command," said Jasper Stripe, and he hurried down the hall to get the TV and the VCR. From her office, Principal Buttle warned him not to run.

While they were waiting, the students pretended a rich curiosity about snowy owls. But really they were worried. What if Mayor Grass had gone to dinner with Widow Wendell? What if she had suddenly seemed wonderful to him? What if *they* had eloped last night?

Love could be a migraine headache.

Jasper Stripe came with the TV and the VCR. Thekla inserted the videotape. She knew there was no segment on the snowy owl recorded there. But she acted as if there were. Once again the neon-colored face of Chad Hunkley blossomed hugely on the screen. But this time Miss Earth didn't complain, because she didn't notice. She was busy admiring how Jasper Stripe was taping down the electric cord to the floor so no one would trip over it. "I do admire a person who's attentive to detail," she muttered, almost to herself.

"I like a person who notices such things," he muttered back, as if talking to the duct tape.

"Fawn," murmured Rhoda, "I think Kos is ready to

137

shoot. He is all warmed up. But if he starts to shiver with the cold, his aim won't be so good. Where is Mayor Grass?"

The door burst open. Mayor Grass strode in. He had a bunch of roses under one arm, and a pile of paperback books stacked up on top. "All the works of Stephanie Queen you haven't read yet," he said to Miss Earth. He slapped the books one by one on her desk. "*Stranded in Siberia, Captive in Cancun,* and *Demented in Detroit.*"

"How about *Lucky in Love*?" said Miss Earth. She didn't even turn her gaze from her dear Jasper Stripe.

"I don't know that one," said Mayor Grass. "Sounds great, though."

Rhoda picked up one of Kos's two arrows. The last chance! She helped the baby cupid raise the bow. She helped him fit the arrow to it. Kos concentrated. He squinted for perfect aim. He let go.

"Ow!" said Miss Earth, clapping her hand on her butt. "More bees! Where are they nesting, in the intercom system?"

To lend credibility to their teacher's theory, all the kids began to buzz, sounding like a swarm of wild bees somewhere in the room.

"Hurry!" said Fawn.

Rhoda grabbed the other arrow. She handed it to Kos, who raised the bow. Rhoda fitted the arrow to it. The baby cupid pulled the string back. He concentrated. He squinted for perfect aim. The children stopped buzzing and held their breaths. Milos and Naxos began to chant softly, "Go! Go! Go! Go! Go!"

"Some bee has the nerve to bother *my* honeybee?" said Jasper Stripe, looking around, ready to rush to Miss Earth's rescue.

"Who are you calling *your* honeybee?" said Mayor Grass quietly. He dropped the roses and the books, and pushed aside the audiovisual cart with the TV and the VCR. Some of the duct tape came up off the floor.

Kos let the last arrow fly. Mayor Grass took a step toward Miss Earth.

The screen of the TV fractured into a thousand pieces. The beautiful face of Chad Hunkley broke up, leaving behind only a puff of smoke.

17

The Couch Potato of Hamlet

Trouble," said Rhoda. "More trouble!" All the cupids dove into the knapsack. Kos began whimpering like a baby hamster.

Jasper Stripe looked around as if he had just woken up to find he had sleepwalked into the ladies' underwear section of a department store. "What the hey?" he muttered. Then he saw the TV monitor with the shattered screen. With undisguised relief he babbled, "I'll just trundle this thing outta your way, Miss Earth. Then I'll get a broom to sweep up this glass. You want me to bring the replacement? It's the little portable I watch *Court TV* on."

"Please," said Miss Earth, not even glancing at Jasper Stripe. "At once, if you don't mind." Her hands went out toward the broken TV monitor.

"Oh, my gosh," hissed Thekla Mustard. "Just when we've changed our minds, she's finally fallen for Chad Hunkley!"

Miss Earth whipped around. "Chad Hunkley!" she said. "Beautiful name. Beautiful man. Did you see how his manly teeth gleamed? Good dental hygiene is a must. Remember this. And his hair, every perfect, jaunty thread of it, cresting like–like–like an asparagus fern! Don't you think a full head of hair is the most convincing part of any newscaster's opinion?"

Mayor Grass's hair, as it happened, was about as thin as it had been when he was four months old. If he had still sported a crest, he would have looked crestfallen. As it was, he blundered on. "Miss Earth!" he exlaimed. "I brought you some books. Your favorite author, Stephanie Queen. Featuring the antics of that zany redhead, Spangles O'Leary."

"Oh, books," said Miss Earth tiredly. "The thing about books is that they're so *heavy*. If you know what I mean."

The children were scandalized. "Miss Earth!" said Pearl Hotchkiss. "You're a card-carrying member of the National Council of Teachers of English! How can you diss books?"

"That stuff about books being good for the mind—it's all a bit overrated, don't you think?" said Miss Earth thinly. She didn't look as if she had much more life than a doughnut right now.

"But look," said Mayor Grass. "I also brought you *Abducted in Arabia*! The very latest. See, it's a double volume, packaged with its sequel, *Quicksanded in Q'om*." He pulled the heavy hardcover from the big pocket of his parka. "They say it's a book that you can't put down."

Miss Earth heaved it onto the desk with a thud. "I say it's a book that you can't pick up."

Mayor Grass continued desperately. "Roses, Miss Earth. I brought you roses. Beautiful roses . . ."

"Roses have thorns," said Miss Earth. "Thorns hurt. TV doesn't hurt."

Mayor Grass couldn't believe his eyes or ears. The children felt terrible. "Here," said Thekla Mustard, rushing forward, "let me put those roses in some water, Mayor Grass. I'm sure Miss Earth will come to her senses in a moment. She's just had a shock."

"Perhaps it's a shock due to a bee sting?" said Mayor Grass. "Let me go ask Nurse Crisp to check her out and administer an antidote, if need be."

"TV is a wonderful antidote to everything," said Miss Earth staunchly.

Mayor Grass left, looking worried. The kids sat at their desks. Jasper Stripe returned with the small black-and-white TV. It didn't have the right fixtures to hook up to the VCR. Miss Earth wasn't going to be able to find Chad Hunkley now, since the *Breakfast in America* show was only on from nine till ten o'clock.

But Miss Earth fiddled with the antenna and worried the knob about. Without the help of a satellite dish, TV reception in rural Vermont was poor. For a while she couldn't tune in to anything much. Still, she made comments about the gray herringbone stripes that zigzagged nervously, east to west. "Soothing, and somehow stimulating, too, don't you agree?" she asked the class.

They nodded as one, more out of dumb disbelief than anything else. The kids began to get even more alarmed. Miss Earth hadn't fallen in love with Chad Hunkley or even the actual TV set he had been seen on, but with *the whole concept of television.*

Finally Miss Earth found a show that was almost coming in. It was either a cooking show or a live broadcast of an Olympic sledding event. The children thought they heard a cultured voice remark, "And then you simply fold the butter into the batter, using your body weight to correct against speeds of up to ninety miles an hour . . ." But they couldn't say for sure.

"One can learn much from TV," said Miss Earth. "I recommend it highly." She pulled the reading rocker into the middle of the room and settled herself down in it. She propped her feet up on the pile of books that Mayor Grass left behind.

"Miss Earth!" cried Sammy Grubb. "You can't put your feet on books!"

"Don't be so puritanical," said Miss Earth. "Do books look you in the face and speak to you? No, they do not. They lie around like old pieces of pie that nobody wants. Whereas TV has this powerful pull, with noise and movement. And you don't have to lift a finger. Look, a commercial. Watch carefully. All of life passes before you in commercials, if you but have the eyes to see."

"Drastic situations call for drastic measures," said Lois

Kennedy the Third. Swift and sure of purpose as a United States Marine, she dove to the front of the room and yanked the TV plug out of the socket.

Miss Earth's pupils—the ones in her eyes, not the ones standing around worrying about her—seemed to be dwindling, like the little white dot in the middle of the TV screen. When the white dot disappeared, Miss Earth sat with her hands on her knees as if she, too, had been unplugged.

"Are we in trouble," said Fawn. *"Catastrophe."*

At that moment Nurse Pinky Crisp and Principal Buttle came bustling in. "First it's a flash frostbite frenzy, now a sinister swarm of bees," said Nurse Crisp. "I'm so glad I quit my job in the Emergency Room at the Montpelier General Hospital and moved here. This work is more rewarding."

"Mayor Grass told us you were ill," said Principal Buttle to Miss Earth. "Then he left in a daze. I heard him muttering, 'Maybe the green hair isn't so bad after all . . .' What's going on here?"

"TV," murmured Miss Earth, as if in a coma.

Nurse Crisp shined a tiny flashlight into each of Miss Earth's beautiful eyes. "Hmm. This is unusual."

"What?" said Principal Buttle.

"Her tear ducts seem full to overflowing, but she's not crying. Wonder why not."

"TV." Miss Earth murmured it like a mantra. "TV. Must see TV."

Miss Earth suddenly lunged for the TV cord and plugged it in again. A commercial blared. The TV commanded: "Right now, for a limited time only, a complete set of the novels of Stephanie Queen! Order now! Now! Call 1-800-555-OUCH!"

"What a good idea!" said Miss Earth. "Why didn't I think of that before?"

"But, Miss Earth!" screeched Thekla Mustard. "You have some Stephanie Queen novels right here at your feet!"

"I think they're better if you order them through the TV," said Miss Earth.

Principal Buttle and Nurse Crisp looked at each other sagely and nodded. "You've finally cracked," said Principal Buttle to Miss Earth. "Being the best teacher in the school has proved too much for you. So let's get you home for a little loving care by your mother." Nurse Crisp and Principal Buttle locked arms with Miss Earth and marched her out of the room.

"For homework, class," Miss Earth called over her shoulder, "watch as much TV as you can, and tell me all about it tomorrow!"

18

Candy Hearts and Poison Darts?

For the rest of the day, Principal Buttle oversaw Miss Earth's class. Since it was too cold to go out at lunchtime, Miss Earth's students had no way to gather in privacy and discuss the disaster. It wasn't until school let out that Fawn could meet her classmates in the schoolyard and open her knapsack to consult again with Rhoda.

"If ever I thought being in love was like being trapped in a magic spell," said Fawn, "this is proof. Miss Earth hates TV. She's not herself. How can we rescue her *now*?"

"We have no more arrows," said Rhoda. "We cupids have failed you." But she didn't sound focused. She kept looking into the recesses of the knapsack at the cupids she was still baby-sitting after all these years.

"We'll work together," said Fawn. "We'll figure out something." But what?

"I am trying to think," said Rhoda. "But I am worried about the boys." The smaller cupids didn't seem healthy. Their skin was more blue than pink.

"Milos! Naxos! Kos!" said Fawn. She peered at them. "Are you asleep? Are you all right?"

The boy cupids were out of it. They looked more like

146

anemic piglets than anything else. Rhoda blinked. "We are slowing down," she said thoughtfully. "I don't know why. Like the naiads murdered in your frozen stream, maybe we spirits of the heart find this place too cold to survive." She closed her eyes and shivered. When humans shiver, it makes them blur a little bit from fast motion. When cupids shiver, it's the opposite. They go slower.

"I've given you hot-water bottles and woolen scarves," said Fawn. "What else can I do?"

"I don't know," murmured Rhoda. "I am feeling too slow to think . . . I can't help you anymore."

"*We'll* help *you*. I promise!" said Fawn. She looked at her classmates. "Don't you think we'd better tell Nurse Crisp? These poor cupids are seriously ill."

"Are you kidding?" said Sammy Grubb. "That'd be the end of them. Nurse Crisp will want to call up the Smithsonian or the National Institute of Science. She'd want the world to know about these newly discovered cupids. She has a scientific mind; it's her professional training. Before you know it, Meg Snoople would be interviewing them on *Breakfast in America!*"

The other kids frowned with worry, nodding in agreement. To let any adults know about the cupids would be a disaster. "Well," said Fawn, "the one thing we can't do is hang around in the cold talking about it. Let's get them home to my house, to the nest in the box near the radiator."

"Everybody think hard," said Thekla Mustard. "When we get to Fawn's house, I'll collect all the ideas, and Sammy and I will sort them out and figure out the best ones."

"Excuse me?" said Pearl Hotchkiss. "I believe I was elected emergency manager of this disaster."

It was a grim trip back to the Hamlet House of Beauty. When the kids got there, Mrs. Petros was sitting in one of her big chairs. She had the footrest up and the headrest back. In her right hand a piece of paper fluttered.

"Hi, Mom," said Fawn. "Some friends came over again, okay?"

"Okay," said her mother in a funny voice.

"What's the matter, Mom?" said Fawn.

"Oh, nothing," said her mother, and she tucked the piece of paper into the pocket of her starched white overblouse. She looked at Fawn fondly. Then she began to laugh.

Fawn was eager to get the cupids back up to their nest, but she didn't know why her mother was laughing. "What is it?" she said.

"I'm not laughing at you," said her mother. "I seem to have done a number on Widow Wendell yesterday. Apparently she got home and—and—her beautiful mop of hair had turned green! Not so bad in itself, but she had bought a new orange dress to wear . . . and it clashed." She was laughing so hard she could hardly speak, and then tears began to spring from her eyes.

Fawn's friends looked on with those blank faces that kids display toward adults exhibiting weird behavior. "Mom," said Fawn, "are you okay?"

Mrs. Petros nodded her head and ducked her face in the apron, waving the children through to the stairwell. "Rice cakes on the counter," she managed to say. And Fawn thought: Is Mom really laughing over the green

hair, or was there something on that piece of paper that has upset her?

Once upstairs, Fawn tucked the boy cupids into their nest, and gently laid Rhoda on her side next to them. "You've taken care of those little ones for these two thousand years and more," murmured Fawn. "Who takes care of you?"

Rhoda didn't reply, but snuggled closer to Milos, Naxos, and Kos. The four of them drifted into sleep, or a kind of half-sleep.

"Dangerously like a coma," observed Pearl.

The children did the best they could. They helped Fawn mound extra blankets and hot-water bottles into a little fort of warmth. But they couldn't tell if it was enough. When Fawn brought the rice cakes to the kids, she tried to feed one to Milos. He was so bleary that he didn't even nibble at it.

Pearl Hotchkiss was raring to go. "Now," she said, "any

ideas on how to break the spell that TV is having over Miss Earth?"

"I don't think the cupids can help," said Sammy Grubb mournfully. "Look at them. They're not much good for anything now."

"You're right. It's up to us," said Lois Kennedy the Third.

"In my heart of hearts," said Salim, "I'd like to blow up all the television sets in Hamlet."

"I know how you feel, but that's not practical," said Pearl. "Besides, we all like to watch reruns of *The Simpsons*."

"How about if we construct our own cupids' arrows out of candy hearts and toy darts?" said Hector Yellow, who liked to make things. "Could we manage to prick Miss Earth with a sweet thought—something that's printed on candy hearts? Like BE MINE or GOOD ENOUGH TO EAT?"

"Are you joking, Hector? That would never work," said Pearl. "For one thing, we're kids, not cupids. For another, you saw how ineffectual the love pencils shot at Sammy and Thekla were, even when aimed by a cupid. Besides, the darts we shot at Miss Earth would probably end up being accidentally poisoned or something. With our luck these days, we'd probably just kill her."

"Could we sponsor a weeklong kick-the-TV-habit campaign?" said Nina Bueno. "Maybe it's like smoking—your lungs begin to recover the day you quit. Maybe Miss Earth will start to come to her senses."

"Not a bad idea," said Pearl, "but that would take a

long time before we knew if it was working. I think we need to be a little more interventionist."

"What's that mean?" said Fawn. She had decided it was a waste of time to pretend you knew something if you didn't, because time was precious now.

"It means we need to interfere more quickly," said Thekla. "Pearl, I know you're the leader of this meeting, but we're not getting anywhere. I'm going to take over."

Pearl began to bristle, but Fawn interrupted. "What if we called up Chad Hunkley? Maybe we could use the TV to get through to Miss Earth. If Miss Earth is home watching TV day and night, she might see him and come to her senses. He could propose to her over the airwaves."

"We'd never get through to him," said Thekla Mustard in a superior tone. "Besides, I've finally realized that people like Chad Hunkley don't want *one* sweetheart—they want *lots* of people to fall in love with them. That's what makes the ratings jump."

"Maybe that's so—" began Fawn.

"It's really a lamebrained idea," said Thekla. "Any others?"

"On the other hand—" said Fawn.

"I think we should move on," said Thekla pointedly.

"Listen to me," said Fawn.

Thekla raised an eyebrow, but she listened.

"We might not care to get through to Chad Hunkley anymore, but we *do* have a connection with Meg Snoople," said Fawn. "Meg interviewed Lois Kennedy the Third on national TV last October when the Siberian snow spiders were on the loose in Hamlet. I bet we could contact Meg Snoople. Get on her show. Miss Earth would be paying attention."

"But then what?" said Thekla.

"Miss Earth has become a TV addict. So we'll find a way to get our message across through TV. Somehow. Wave posters in the background. Jump up and down. We'll, like, think of something. That's a later stage of the plan."

Thekla looked doubtful. But Pearl Hotchkiss was grinning. "That's a brilliant idea!" said Pearl.

"Hey, Fawn, sounds like a winner!" said Sammy Grubb.

"Just pick up the phone," Fawn said to Lois Kennedy the Third, "and ask directory assistance for the *Breakfast in America* show. I think it broadcasts out of New York."

"Aren't we even going to vote on this?" said Thekla Mustard, in a huff.

But the feeling in the room was so positive that no one even bothered to answer her. Lois Kennedy the Third, who liked taking the lead over Thekla Mustard whenever there was the chance, was already on the phone. She was saying, "The number for Meg Snoople, Human Interest Department, the *Breakfast in America* show. And make it snappy."

An Emergency Book Report

Lois Kennedy the Third got Meg Snoople on the phone in three minutes flat.

"I bet you know a good human-interest story when you smell one," said Lois bluntly. "Our teacher, Miss Earth, was featured on your show last year. You covered a story about her being bit by a spider, and how she recovered. But now she's fallen ill. She can't do anything but stay home and watch TV. And we miss her."

There was a silence as Lois listened to Meg Snoople try to weasel out of it.

"You're not paying attention," said Lois patiently. "You met Miss Earth last fall when she was bit by a *Siberian snow spider*. For your loyal viewers—who, as we all know, number in the millions—this episode will be a follow-up. A return to small-town values. A little ninety-second segment to warm the heartstrings of America. Let us be on your show to send our love to our poor suffering teacher. We're talking a three-hankie moment here. You know we are."

Lois was good. She listened, she nodded, and then she hung up. Her classmates said, "Well?"

"Last year's spider scare gave Meg Snoople's career a big boost. She likes the idea of returning to Hamlet," said

Lois. "She said if we did what she asked, we could expect her helicopter by nine A.M. tomorrow. She said to make sure the kindergartners were safely inside. As a national TV personality, she has more important things to worry about than kindergartners getting swept off their feet by the high winds raised by helicopter propellers."

"Good job," said Sammy. "What did she ask us to do?"

"Before she schedules a 'Return to Hamlet' sequence, she needs to talk to some grownup in authority."

"We'll get Mayor Grass to call her," said Pearl. "As mayor, he's responsible for public relations for Hamlet."

"He's rather shy. Would he talk to Meg Snoople?" asked Lois.

"He has Miss Earth's best interests at heart," said Pearl. "Fawn, do you want to ask him?"

Fawn shook her head. Sammy Grubb said, "I'll go. Why not. I'll have a man-to-man talk with him."

"If *you're* going to do it, that would be a man-to-twerp talk," said Thekla Mustard.

"Well, if you did it, it wouldn't be a talk at all, because you never shut up," Sammy Grubb replied. "It'd be a man-stupefied-into-silence-by-a—"

"Enough," said Fawn, Lois, Salim, Hector, Nina, Moshe, Stan, Carly, Sharday, Anna Maria, Mike, Forest Eugene, and Pearl, all at the same time. Sammy and Thekla glowered at each other, as if no one else but they understood the crushing demands of leadership.

"Mayor Grass will call Meg Snoople. She'll come. It's that simple," stated Lois. "I could tell she was very interested. Little does she know she's the antidote to TV obsession. We're fighting fire with fire, as the saying goes."

"I wish I could light a fire to warm these cupids," said Fawn, who was kneeling down next to them. She wanted to pick them up and cradle them like dolls, but she thought it would be undignified. Even though they were small, they were not pets or toys. Yet didn't they deserve to be held and loved, too? Didn't everybody?

She knew the answer to that question. *Yes*. So she reached in and gently stroked their foreheads and hummed to them.

"Well," said Thekla Mustard, "the next part of the plan is the difficult part. We have to think of something persuasive to say to Miss Earth on TV, especially if it's going to be broadcast nationally as well. We have our own reputations to maintain. After all, I may be headed for the White House, and someday this footage can be used in my election campaign."

The friends spent the next hour brainstorming a strategy. How to communicate with Miss Earth? Posters? A skit? A class song? Fawn tried to pay attention. But she was so worried that the cupids were freezing to death.

After an hour, the classmates still couldn't decide on how best to use the airtime. Every idea got voted down. The students left for home with instructions to call in new ideas to Pearl Hotchkiss, coordinator of this campaign. "Everybody think hard. Don't be stupid," said Thekla, as they left.

"Don't say *stupid*," said everyone, one by one.

Fawn tried to think, too. But she was worried about so many things. About her mother . . . laughing and crying over a *letter*? Had that only been a note from Widow Wendell, complaining about green hair? Or had it been something else?

It was dark, the close-fitting early dark of a winter afternoon. Some of the windows in the buildings in the center of Hamlet were lit with incandescent bulbs behind yellow shades, some with the cool white of fluorescence. The light spilled out over the heaps of snow, making the black-purple sky seem more black, more purple. The center of town was pleasantly noxious with the fumes from cars left with their engines running as their drivers ran into Clumpett's General Store for last-minute supper ingredients.

Sammy Grubb approached the town garage, a big white wooden shed that housed the town's fire engine, a snowplow, a dump truck, and a tractor. Mayor Grass could often be found here, in a little heated booth with a rocker and a radio. But today the windows were dark. Mayor Grass wasn't there. Nor was he in the library. Finally Sammy located him near the meat counter in Clumpett's. Mayor Grass was selecting some choice bologna and some Vermont cheddar cheese. Sammy tramped his wet boots across the sawdusty floorboards to the back of the store.

"Mayor Grass," said Sammy. "I have to ask your help."

"A school project? I'm your man," said Mayor Grass. "What can I do for you, Sammy?"

"It's about Miss Earth," said Sammy.

Bucky Clumpett glanced up from the sausage-stuffing machine. His wife, Olympia, peered across the carton of toilet paper she was unpacking. Widow Wendell withdrew her head from the freezer case and looked chilly. "Let's go outside," said Mayor Grass.

The mayor of Hamlet, Vermont, and the Chief of the Copycats Club stood on the snowy walkway of the porch. They shuffled nervously, to keep warm, grinding under their boots the little bits of kitty litter that were used to prevent folks from slipping on the ice. "So, what's your problem?" said Mayor Grass at last.

Sammy had spent some time thinking over his strategy. "I don't know if you're very concerned about the health and welfare of my teacher, Miss Earth," said Sammy in a conversational tone.

"I take a passing interest," said Mayor Grass guardedly. He stared across the green to the front of the Congregational/Unitarian Church. "After all, she is an employee of the town. I'd be lost without her."

"You would?" said Sammy with a gleam in his eye.

"I mean, as mayor, of course," he went on to explain. "Officially. I'm duty-bound to care. It's part of the job description on file in the town clerk's office."

"Miss Earth seems to be having a bad time of it these days," said Sammy. "I don't know why. Valentine's Day blues, I guess."

"Roses are red, violets are blue," said Mayor Grass. "She still pines for Senator Tortoni."

Sammy Grubb said, "Who?"

"Didn't you know? She was engaged to a senator from

157

New York. What a pretty couple they made! And he was killed in that freak accident—"

"—involving a Santa Claus float, I know, I know," said Sammy. "But I never knew he was a *senator*."

"Who could ever hope to measure up?" said Mayor Grass. "He was perfect, and he's dead. I'm alive and imperfect, getting more imperfect with every passing day. He was handsome. I'm a hayseed. He was classy. I am clueless. He was a senator, for crying out loud."

"You're a mayor," said Sammy encouragingly.

"Not really," said Mayor Grass. "Haven't you done local civics yet? Hamlet is too small a town to have a real mayor. People just call me that as a long-running polite joke, a mock honorific. I'm really only Timothy Grass, chairperson of the Board of Selectmen. And I ask you: How could Miss Earth go from loving a senator to loving a selectman? Who could blame her for resisting me?"

Sammy Grubb hadn't expected the conversation to take quite this turn. But he wasn't Chief of the Copycats for nothing. He could improvise. He rummaged in his knapsack and said, "Here, Mayor Grass. In case you want to use it. Nothing more powerful than a valentine from a secret admirer, if you ask me."

Mayor Grass looked at it.

> Love is love. Like is like.
> Love is scary. Like is not.
> Love is yucky. Like is lucky.
> Someone likes you quite a lot.
>
> A secret admirer

"I'm not sure I understand," said Mayor Grass. "Are you giving me a valentine, Sammy? Are you a secret admirer of mine?"

"Mayor Grass," said Sammy, taking a deep breath and trying again, "my admiration for you is anything but secret. I am a public booster, and I'm trying to give you a suggestion. Erase my name on the outside of this card and replace it with 'Miss Earth.' Then give it to her. You'll thank me for it. Only, please don't thank me in public. I'd never live it down if it got around that *I* was playing cupid."

"I see," said Mayor Grass. He read the valentine again. "Thanks, Sammy. I'll think about it." And he put it in his pocket.

Sammy then launched into the real reason for the meeting. He needed Mayor Grass to phone Meg Snoople and confirm the invitation to Hamlet. "Okay, I'll get right on it," said Mayor Grass hastily. He could see Widow Wendell paying for her groceries. Sprightly spikes of green hair were escaping from underneath her tightly wound headscarf. He was eager to escape before Widow Wendell emerged from Clumpett's General Store. He lit out from the porch, calling over his shoulder, "You can count on me, Sammy. I'll make that call and be as persuasive as I can manage."

"You're a *good mayor*," said Sammy loudly. "It's a matter of public record." But he hoped he hadn't just handed Mayor Grass the equivalent of a poison dart.

Fawn laid out her clothes for school tomorrow. She was supposed to wear red. Thekla Mustard had said that red would show up best on a color TV. Besides, red was the color of love. Fawn chose red snowpants and a sort of reddish pink sweatshirt that said: ANTARCTICA: RELAX. ENJOY. CHILL OUT. Beneath the words, two penguins in white stitching were looking at each other with little apparent interest.

All that night, while Fawn sat up and kept a watch over the cupids, she thought about Miss Earth watching TV. Hadn't Miss Earth loved books more than anything? She was always trying to get the kids to read. Sad thing. Then Fawn remembered that Miss Earth had liked the sound of the Stephanie Queen books once she heard about them on TV. Maybe they could get through to her that way!

In the early morning, when it was still dark out, Fawn crept downstairs into the beauty salon. She wanted to use the telephone without her mother hearing. She dialed Pearl Hotchkiss. She guessed that Pearl would be up already, because Pearl had six younger brothers and sisters. Pearl often said she got up early to do homework because the house was quiet. Sure enough, the phone only rang once, and Pearl's voice was saying in a hushed way, "Hello?"

"Pearl, it's Fawn," said Fawn. She explained her idea. *A book report on national TV* . . .

"Brilliant," said Pearl. "It's the best idea anyone has phoned in yet."

"What are the other ideas?" said Fawn.

"There aren't any," said Pearl.

"Can you write the book report?" said Fawn.

"I could," said Pearl, "but so could you, Fawn."

"No, I can't," said Fawn, and then she corrected herself. "Well, maybe I could, but not today. I'm too worried about the cupids."

"All right, then. You take care of the cupids," said Pearl. "I know Sammy and the boys are trying to glue the broken vase together. So they're pretty busy. And Thekla and the girls are going to explain to Principal Buttle that a major national newscaster is coming to film children at the Josiah Fawcett Elementary School. So I guess this is my job. I'll do what I can, and I'll have the report ready by eight thirty A.M. We may pull this off, Fawn!"

"Okay," said Fawn.

"By the way," said Pearl kindly, "you have been pretty patient with everybody's needling you about being dumb."

"Dumb means you have a hard time talking," said Fawn. "It doesn't mean stupid. I'm not stupid, and I'm not dumb. Sometimes I'm shy, though." And since she was feeling shy, she put the phone down without saying good-bye.

But before she went back upstairs, she saw something on the floor. It was the small piece of paper her mother had been clutching. It must have fallen out of her pocket. Fawn picked it up. It was written in her dad's handwriting. There wasn't much on the paper. It said:

> I've thought about what you said on the phone. I suppose you're right. We have to accept that things are the way they are.

I wonder how Fawn is going to deal with the news?

As always,
Dimitri

As always. As always *what*? As always, I'm far away? As always, I choose to live with my penguins rather than with my family?

Fawn wasn't very good at what Miss Earth called reading comprehension. But it sounded to Fawn as if her dad were saying that he and her mother had to accept that they lived apart. And Fawn was going to have to deal with the news that nothing was going to change.

Do you know what distance means? It means *"quite a lot of far."*

She straightened her shoulders. She wouldn't cry. The cupids needed her care. She pulled the cupids nearer to the radiator in her room and hid them under her sleeping bag, leaving a space for the air to circulate so they wouldn't suffocate.

In the campaign to save their teacher, Miss Earth's students were now entirely on their own. And it was the coldest day of the winter so far.

Principal Buttle was ecstatic. She asked the younger children to make rows of saluting snowmen to greet Meg Snoople and the camera crew. The children were glad to help. They donated scarves and hats to make the snowmen look more welcoming.

Jasper Stripe sprinkled the steps with rock salt so that Meg Snoople wouldn't slip and split her pretty head open. Ms. Frazzle looped her morning kindergarten students together by tying the ends of their scarves so that no stray child could escape and wander onto the makeshift helicopter landing pad. It would spoil the atmosphere if by accident some innocent blood was spilled.

Pearl Hotchkiss briefed Sammy Grubb and Thekla Mustard about the plan. In turn they spoke to their club members. All of Miss Earth's students were ready. They wore red blouses, crimson and scarlet skirts, magenta shirts, and carmine trousers. An abundance of red plaid. Lots of red hats and gloves and coats. Some red rubber boots, too.

"Red, red, ready," said Thekla Mustard, inspecting each of her fellow students.

Promptly at eight fifty-five, a distant rumble over the hills became a nearby roar in the schoolyard. Like a huge flying loaf of bread wrapped in aluminum foil, the helicopter set down. All the saluting snowmen were blown to bits.

Miss Earth's class was lined up on the front steps of the school, shivering and smiling. Meg Snoople leaped out of the helicopter, and she deftly ducked under its whirling blades, making a beeline for the school. Her cameraman followed, and a person holding a big mike. Covered in blue fur, the mike looked like a puppet that had wandered off the set of Sesame Street.

"We haven't got much time. We go live in ninety seconds," said Meg Snoople as the sound of the helicopter's engines faded. "Who's in charge here?"

"Principal Hetty Buttle, at your service!" said

Principal Buttle. She saluted, but since she was dressed in sensible rubber-soled boots from the L. L. Bean catalog, the click of her heels was sadly muffled.

Meg Snoople was efficient. It was one of her job qualifications. "We open on Principal Buttle, saluting my arrival. I say, 'Here we are, blah blah.' We pan to the children. Who's the spokesperson for the kids?"

There was a bit of a scuffle. Finally Salim Bannerjee was pushed forward. "I am Salim Bannerjee, the newest pupil in the school, arrived only in September from India," he said. "I won the vote."

"His voice sort of has an English accent," explained Lois Kennedy the Third. "It'll be very effective. Trust me."

"Love it. You can do your shtick in forty seconds? Camera, selected head shots of kids looking worried. Salim, I'll cut you off if you get boring. Don't take it personally. Kids, lose the red hats, you look stupid."

"Don't say stupid!" shouted all the children.

"Oh," said Meg Snoople. She wasn't used to being talked back to. "I meant dorky."

"That's better," said Fawn. The children all took off their red hats.

"Marks, fifteen seconds," said the cameraman.

"Sound check," said the sound man.

Meg Snoople ran a brush through her hair, which somehow made her hairdo appear more attentive. She lifted her collar rakishly and tucked her chin down. In a tired voice, as if she'd said it every day for ten years, she yammered, "How do I love thee? Let me count the ways.

I love thee to the depth and breadth and height my soul can reach . . ."

"Levels good," said the sound man.

"Light good," said the cameraman. "Keep the mark. Live in *ten. Nine. Eight. Seven. Six.*" Then he held up one hand and silently folded back one finger at a time, indicating *five. Four. Three. Two. One.*

Then with a swooping motion, he pointed at Meg Snoople, who suddenly looked more alive than she had up till then.

"I'm reporting today from the steps of the Joseph Foster School in Hamlet, Vermont," said Meg Snoople, beaming brightly. "Folks in Vermont may be simple, but they're not simple-minded. Let's *find out more*." She turned and strode with athletic grace to where Principal Buttle was standing woodenly, saluting her.

"Good morning, Principal Buttle. I understand you've a problem on your hands."

"It's the *Josiah Fawcett* School," said Principal Buttle, who in matters of public relations was answerable to the school committee. "And we do have a problem. One of our teachers, Miss Earth, is home sick. And her students are heartsick."

"Valentine's Day was scarcely a week ago," said Meg Snoople, turning back to the camera and ignoring Principal Buttle, who stood there as if posing for an oil painting. Meg Snoople hurried on. "Did Miss Earth teach her children anything about the nature of true love? What about the love of students for their teacher? Let's *find out more*." Again she strode briskly a few steps until she was in the center of a clutch of red-clad schoolchildren. "Hi, there, kids. What do you want to share with your teacher today?"

Salim stepped forward. He held the paragraph Pearl had written that morning. He said, "Miss Earth is a good teacher because she teaches us that reading is better for you than watching TV."

"Well," said Meg Snoople, "I don't know if the facts support such a—"

Salim plowed on. "We wrote a book report of a new book we believe Miss Earth would like. If she's listening, perhaps she'll take note. The book is by Stephanie Queen. It's called *Heartbroken in Hamlet*."

"Why, I love Stephanie Queen's work! I intend to read one of her books someday!" said Meg Snoople brightly. "Anyway, I like the TV miniseries they make out of them. Well, that's about all the time we—"

Salim would not be shut up. He said, "Let's *find out more*." He started to read what Pearl had written, even though Stephanie Queen had never written such a book yet and possibly never would.

"In *Heartbroken in Hamlet,* this is a book where Spangles O'Leary, the heroine, moves to Hamlet, Vermont. She gets a job as a teacher in a grade school. It's really exciting because the teacher gets put under a spell, and she falls in love with TV of any kind."

"How novel," said Meg Snoople, making a joke of it. She laughed so that ten million viewers would laugh along with her. They probably did.

Salim didn't laugh. "But TV poisons the mind. It drains the soul. It turns willpower to frozen sludge," he continued. "So the only way Spangles O'Leary can be saved is when she gets trapped in a burning library and has to consult a book to find out how to extinguish a fire. Then she remembers how important books are. It's kind of symbolic—the burning books and all. And when she saves the books with a bucket of water, she saves herself from the spell of evil TV. I like this book because it's really interesting. I recommend it to anyone who likes good books."

"I'll have to try it," said Meg Snoople, indicating with her left hand that the helicopter pilot should start up the propellers again. Later in the show she had to do another live segment. "This is Meg Snoople—"

"I'm not done," said Salim.

All the children leaned forward and cupped their hands around their mouths. They shouted: "Miss Earth! We love you! We miss you! Come back to us!"

Meg Snoople looked taken aback. For a moment her face softened. "Isn't that sweet," she murmured. "I think these children have learned something this morning. And *haven't we all*. Now, after the commercial break, rejoin *Breakfast in America*. My co-anchor, Chad Hunkley, will interview a man in Nebraska who has taught his parrots to sing 'A Bicycle Built for Two' in four-part harmony." She held a smile of delighted anticipation until the cameraman said, "And—you're clear."

"Parrots singing barbershop quartets!" she said blisteringly. "Sometimes, kids, I think your teacher has got the right idea about television!"

The children could only nod in agreement. Had they been able to use TV itself to break the spell of TV? A spell even stronger than love? . . . It was their only hope.

The helicopter took the film crew away, Meg Snoople waving through the curved glass. Principal Buttle finally relaxed. Mayor Grass appeared at the outside door of Miss Earth's classroom—had he been watching the broadcast on the TV in there? He gave Sammy Grubb a thumbs-up salute as he crossed the schoolyard, heading for his truck.

Mrs. Cobble, the school secretary, waved her arms from the front door. She bellowed, "Principal Buttle, there's a phone call for you in the office. It's Miss Earth."

Principal Buttle broke her own rules. At top speed, she ran up the slope, into the school, and down the corridor to take the call.

20

Frozen and Unfrozen

By the time the children reached the school office, Principal Buttle had already hung up. She had a down-to-earth look on her face. "Children, back to your classroom," she told them. "I believe that Miss Earth is on her way to work."

The kids settled at their desks. They looked to Thekla Mustard, Empress of the Tattletales, and to Sammy Grubb, Chief of the Copycats, for instruction. They looked to Pearl Hotchkiss, director of this disaster management campaign, for help.

But it was Fawn Petros who spoke up. "Maybe we should read until Miss Earth gets here," she said. And that seemed as good an idea as any.

In fact—because books have a peculiar power to take you both into and out of yourself—a number of eyes blinked with surprise when Miss Earth arrived.

"Good morning, Miss Earth," recited the class.

"Good morning, children," said Miss Earth briskly, in her best let's-get-to-work-but-not-at-the-expense-of-enjoying-life voice. "Glad to see you're reading. Always carry a paperback with you in your knapsack, my pets. You never know when an elevator is going to get stuck between floors and hold you up for an hour or so. A good book can help you pass the time. It improves your mind as well."

This sounded like the Miss Earth they knew. Because it was.

She continued. "I had a funny dream," she said. "I don't know why. Perhaps it was a reaction to all the commotion over Valentine's Day this year. I seemed to be falling in love with everything and everyone I ran across. I even had a few rapid heartbeats over something I saw on TV!"

"Chad Hunkley?" asked Thekla Mustard. She couldn't help herself.

"That Neanderthal?" scoffed Miss Earth. "He's already in love—with himself. No, I dreamed that my wonderful students were on the *Breakfast in America* show, telling me they loved me. And I woke up, and it was late. I'm sorry to be tardy. But glad to see you're all reading." She looked at the TV in the front of the room. "What is this doing here?" She walked right up to it. She stared into the TV screen, which stood on the audiovisual cart exactly high enough so that she could look in it like a mirror.

Miss Earth murmured, "Mirror, mirror, on the wall, what do we see in you at all?"

A piece of paper was taped to the front of the TV. Only Sammy Grubb and Pearl Hotchkiss could guess what it said, but Pearl had no idea how it had gotten there. Miss Earth removed the note, unfolded it, and read it. "A welcome-back message from someone anonymous," she said. "How nice."

Then she shoved the whole cart out the door into the hallway. "Jasper Stripe can take this back where it belongs," she said. "Now, class, I'm in the mood for book reports. Anybody want to talk about what you've read lately that you really love?"

But before anyone could reply, there was a knock on the door. Miss Earth said in a comic voice, "Chad Hunkley, I presume?" Then, in a normal voice, she called, "Come in!"

The door opened. In walked Mayor Tim Grass.

"Excuse me, children," he said. "I was on my way to the town garage, but I turned back. I have something urgent to say to Miss Earth. In person, not in an anonymous note. I have decided to be brave."

"Please, don't mind us," said Thekla Mustard. "Go right ahead. We'll just read."

"Class, excuse me for a moment," said Miss Earth. She stepped out into the hallway. But the door was open. All the students leaned forward on their desks and cupped their hands around their ears to hear.

"Maybe you can learn a few things from TV, after all," said Mayor Grass.

"I doubt it," answered Miss Earth.

"Well, I heard something said on TV this morning that I want to repeat," said Mayor Grass.

"I hope it's educational," said Miss Earth, a bit sniffily.

"I hope so, too," said Mayor Grass. He took Miss Earth's hands in his. He said something in a low voice. None of the kids could hear it.

"Darn!" said Lois. "What's he saying?"

"Be my bloody valentine?" said Sammy Grubb.

"Be my sweet patootie?" said Thekla Mustard.

"Someone likes you quite a lot?" said Pearl Hotchkiss, hoping that Sammy Grubb would recognize the quote and realize that it was she and not Lois who had sent him the secret admirer's valentine. But her hint zoomed right over his head.

"Come home to me?" whispered Fawn Petros.

"Miss Earth, you are one hot item?" suggested Sharday Wren.

"Let's make beautiful music together?" said Anna Maria Mastrangelo, and sang a few notes of "Love Makes the World Go Round."

But before the rest of the kids could come up with their own ideas, Miss Earth poked her head inside the open doorway. "Work on your book reports till I return," said Miss Earth firmly. Then she closed the door for a little privacy. Maybe she and Mayor Grass went for a stroll down the hall to the cafeteria.

She still wasn't back ten minutes later when Jasper Stripe came to take the TV away. Fawn wondered: What might *he* might think about the situation? In his terrarium, Kermit the Hermit was staring unblinkingly ahead as usual. And, Fawn mused, maybe, far, far up in the stratosphere, Meg Snoople's helicopter was passing by a balloon figure of Cap'n Trueheart orbiting the globe. If Meg Snoople wasn't too busy fixing her lipstick for the next live segment, maybe she could look out the window and see if Cap'n Trueheart approved.

21

Happy in Hamlet

At recess, the boys took out the Greek jug. They showed the girls how far they'd gotten in reconstructing it. The bottom third was all put together. "How did you replace the missing pieces?" asked Thekla Mustard.

"We borrowed some modeling clay from our kindergarten buddies," said Sammy Grubb. "The little kids are good at making clay snakes, and the snakes serve as good joiners between the broken pieces. A little peanut butter finishes the job."

"Impressive," Thekla murmured. "Why don't you do the rest?"

"We think that the cupids might be too tired to squeeze in through the narrow opening," said Sammy. "We thought maybe we should first set them inside and then build the jug up around them."

"Sounds an awful lot like a clay coffin," said Thekla Mustard. The others had to agree.

"But what else can we do?" asked Sammy.

"Not sure," said Thekla.

"We'd better do something fast. I'm terribly worried that they're dying," said Fawn. "They need to go home."

Mrs. Brill, the lunch lady, came up to the children on their snowbank. "Fawn, your mother just called to say you'd better get home fast. Family situation. I've cleared it with the office."

"I'll get your homework, Fawn," said Sharday Wren.

"I'll bring your books," said Stan Tomaski.

"We'll come this afternoon and finish the jug," said Sammy Grubb.

"Okay," said Fawn. She was glad to have friends, but she was worried about being called home in the middle of the day. This had never happened before. Maybe her mother was having a slow morning; maybe she'd left the salon and wandered upstairs into Fawn's bedroom to tidy up. Maybe she'd found the cupids at last. One problem after another. What next?

When she got to the Hamlet House of Beauty, the sign on the door said CLOSED, though lunchtime was usually the busiest hour. Fawn ran past the two haircutting chairs and the hair-washing station. Black curls were all over the floor. Her mother hadn't even swept them up. That wasn't like her.

From upstairs came a smell of fresh coffee and gently burning bacon. Moving more slowly, Fawn climbed the steps. "Mom?" she began, and turned the corner at the top of the stairs into the kitchen.

"—and Dad," she finished in a weak voice.

There he was, in a thermal undershirt and jeans and a year's worth of beard. He was sitting on a kitchen chair, with Mrs. Petros across from him.

He looked up. "Look who's here!" he said. He jumped up from his chair, and Fawn was in his arms, and he was in hers. She was lifted off the floor, like a little baby, like a pet, like a beloved toy, like a bunch of flowers. A daughter in the arms of her father. Swung around and around, a small whirlwind of amazement.

When she had stopped crying for joy, Fawn said, "Is this just a visit?"

"No," said Mr. Petros. "I love you. I've come back to you."

Mrs. Petros put out an early lunch of eggs and bacon. She and her husband beamed at each other. They drank cup after cup of coffee. Fawn didn't touch her milk or do much more than nibble at her toast. She couldn't eat. She was too happy to eat.

Fawn's classmates stopped by after school. It wasn't the best possible timing for the Petros family. But Mr. Petros said, "Come on in, guys and gals. Troop right on through. Fawn's in her bedroom. I have to unpack and sort my polar gear, anyway. Gonna sell some of it, and polish the rest and hang it on the wall. Antarctica's a bitter place, my lads, coldest place on earth, and if you can survive that cold, you can survive—"

"Wait," said Moshe Cohn, pausing on his way to Fawn's room. "How did you survive such awful cold, Mr. Petros?"

"Having a warm heart, my friend," he answered.

Moshe rolled his eyes. "No, really," he said.

"Well, that and some good thermal underwear. That's what helps humans. But other creatures of the terrain sometimes go into a deep sleep, like a hibernation. The cold slows them down, but it doesn't kill them. When the weather warms up again—or as warm as it gets down there—they warm up right along with it. Nature's way of ensuring survival."

"But didn't you miss your family?" said Thekla.

"Of course I did. That's why I came back. I got a wonderful valentine faxed from Fawn. And a phone call from my pretty wife. I couldn't live without them. I'm a scientist, but I'm not a penguin. And I'm not frozen."

Mrs. Petros smiled.

"Also my funding got cut," said Mr. Petros. "I'm applying for a job as a research associate over at Dartmouth College."

The children had heard enough. They went into Fawn's bedroom. They peered into the nesting box. Milos, Naxos, and Kos were curled up near each other.

Fawn had Rhoda in her hands. She was stroking her head as if Rhoda were a sickly kitten. "You should have heard what my dad just told us about animals in the arctic winter," she said. "He's very smart, you know. Maybe, like animals in the cold, you aren't dying. Maybe you're just hibernating."

"Hey," said Moshe. "Fawn, you're pretty smart, too. Maybe you're right."

Rhoda stirred a bit and opened her eyes. She had the smallest, faintest smile. "Even if we die," she whispered, "love doesn't die. Don't you know that? Sometimes it falls asleep. But it always wakes up again."

"And so will you," said Fawn. "Rhoda, listen to me. Streams thaw in the spring here. Did we ever remember to tell you that? If there are naiad spirits there, they wake up, I bet. The ice melts. The sun warms the earth."

Rhoda whispered something so low that Fawn had to lean very close to hear. Rhoda said, "I miss my home, my mother, my girlfriends the naiads. But you've been my good friend while I've been here, and that's love enough for me. Thank you, dear heart."

Fawn blinked back wetly. She said, "You're not going to die. You're immortal, remember? Now, we can't carry you in our knapsacks to Greece, or ride you there in the school bus. You can't fly yourselves there. So we're going to send you back to Greece the way you got here. By airmail, with LOVE stamps all over the box. And when you

177

get to Athens, my aunt Sophia will take a train north and carry the jug to Mount Olympus and open it. I'll write her to tell her to do this. And then you can all go home to your mothers."

Rhoda smiled as if she were having a lovely dream of home, of olive trees and sunny mountain slopes, and the music of lyres and pipes, and the chatter of the naiads, and the flowery scent of her mother's love.

And of saying bye-bye to the three other cupids.

"And, Rhoda," whispered Fawn. "Thank *you*."

Fawn straightened her spine. She took the red pincushion that Mayor Grass had given to Miss Earth, and she set it inside the jug as a souvenir for Rhoda. On it she had written in felt-tip marker I ❤ VERMONT.

"Let's close 'em up," she said, and the children got to work.

The next day was Saturday. Fawn and her mother made blueberry pancakes and a large pot of coffee for her father, since he was jetlagged and sleepy still. The three of them sat in the winter sunlight, talking about what could happen next. Anything could happen next. Going to the movies over in Hanover? Buying some new paint to redecorate Fawn's bedroom? Being together as a family forever and ever? They all sounded like good ideas to Fawn.

After breakfast, Mrs. Petros helped Fawn put the Greek vase in a huge carton and surround it with bubble wrap and Styrofoam peanuts. "Are you sure Aunt Sophia will understand why you're sending her present back?" said Mrs. Petros.

"I wrote a letter explaining it," said Fawn. "It's kind of a class project."

"This is impressive, how you've dripped candle wax in the mouth of the jug to keep it closed. However, I think your Aunt Sophia will still see that it got broken."

"Oh, well. Things get broken, and then they get fixed."

"Like hearts?" said Mrs. Petros, a little dreamily.

"Like vases," said Fawn firmly.

"Maybe," said Mrs. Petros. "Anyway, I still think it could make a decent lamp base, if you had a lampshade with a lot of fringe."

Mr. Petros and Fawn put on their overcoats. "Heaps of snow in Vermont this year," said Mr. Petros. "Looks an awful lot like Antarctica."

"Right," said Fawn. "Huge snowfall this winter. They say Killington and the other ski slopes are having a record season."

As they walked to the post office, Mr. Petros sang an old song about spring and love and other romantic things. The world looked glorious, snowy hills and bare trees and ice-choked streams. Fawn almost started to sing with her dad, but she didn't. She just liked to hear his voice by itself. They'd have plenty of time to sing together.

Mr. Petros stopped singing at Clumpett's General Store. On Saturdays, the post office window at the back of Clumpett's was open from eight until noon. The post-mistress—Sharday Wren's older sister, Kanesha—weighed the box carefully and added extra strapping tape for good measure. She gave Mr. Petros the customs forms. "Want any insurance in case it breaks?" she asked.

"What do you think it's worth?" said Mr. Petros to Fawn.

"To some people," said Fawn seriously, "it's worth just about everything."

"And to you?" said her father.

"Well," said Fawn, "what's inside is pretty important. But it's not anything you could replace with money. The best things never are, are they?" She thought of the cupids, and she thought of her parents. She grinned at her dad and licked some stamps and pounded them on the box so hard that the vase would have broken all over again if it hadn't been wrapped and packed so well.

And that's almost the end of it, but there's just a bit more.

On Saturday afternoon, Miss Earth did a little house-cleaning. She found the black-and-white photo of Rocco Tortoni in a drawer, and she set it on the sideboard. "I'm not ready to put it away for good," she said to her mother, "for I will always love my Rocco. But I can love other people, too."

Grandma Earth nodded, and was wise enough not to make any remarks at all.

The following week, Miss Earth finished her reading aloud of classic fairy tales. The children did book reports on fairy tales. Frankly, they were getting sick and tired of fairy tales, but they didn't want to complain. They just were glad to have their teacher back to her senses.

The children had to write a fantastic story as the final project in the fairy tale unit. The story didn't have to be a fairy tale, but it had to have some magical element in it. The kids worked hard for several days, and over the weekend Miss Earth read their stories.

She came in to school the following Monday. "They were all excellent," she said. "But my favorite was Fawn's."

Fawn wasn't used to a remark like this. But this story had come out easily. "I wrote it myself, Miss Earth," she said. "Though I admit my mom and my dad, like, helped me with the spelling."

"Very smart of you to ask for help when you need it," said Miss Earth. "I'll read this story to the class in a minute. It's imaginative, even a bit zany. I just have one question, Fawn. It's about the title. You call it 'Four Stupid Cupids.' I can see you like the sound of rhyming words. But why not call it 'Four Torpid Cupids'? Torpid means 'slowed down,' and by the end, with the cupids so cold and still, you could say they were torpid."

"I like 'Four Stupid Cupids,'" said Fawn.

"But don't you think that title is—perhaps—a bit mean-spirited? These cupids aren't incapable of knowledge. They're just ignorant—which is from a Latin word meaning 'not knowing.' The cupids didn't know that Vermont's cold winter isn't permanent."

Fawn was silent for a moment. She tried to line up her words in her head before saying them. She made a little picture in her mind, three speech balloons, with three thoughts written out, one in each balloon. Everyone waited.

When she was ready, she spoke. "You're right, Miss Earth. The cupids aren't really stupid. But don't you think *stupid* means different things? Sometimes we say people are stupid when we mean that they're not too bright. And sometimes we say people are stupid just because we don't like them and it's a lazy way to admit it. But sometimes we call things—or people—or events—stupid to disguise the fact that we just don't know much about them."

"I never call anything stupid," said Thekla Mustard hotly.

"That's a stupid remark," said Sammy Grubb.

Fawn went on. "I agree with Miss Earth. *Stupid* is an ugly word. But that's the point of my story. Until you know about something, you think it's stupid."

"Give me an example," said Miss Earth.

Fawn hadn't thought of any examples. But a picture of Rhoda flew up in her mind. Rhoda was smiling at her and shooting an arrow in Fawn's direction, as if to give her a sting of inspiration.

"For instance," said Fawn. "To kids, *love* seems sort of stupid. But once you realize what it is, it seems like the smartest thing on earth." The picture of Rhoda faded. Fawn was now thinking of her dad smiling at her.

"Fawn," said Miss Earth. "I do believe you're right."

Miss Earth looked down at her finger. The children noticed she was wearing a small ring that hadn't been there before. An engagement ring? A going-steady ring? A just-friends ring? A ring from a box of Cracker Jacks? They couldn't tell.

The children were rarely shy around their teacher. Miss Earth was rarely shy around her students. But just for a moment the silence was full of tender shyness. Then a loud clump of snow fell off a pine tree just outside the classroom windows. It made everyone jump. Dots of snow flew up, and the strengthening sunlight sent hundreds of brilliant miniature rainbows flickering all over the classroom.

"Snow's melting. The earth is warming up," said Miss Earth. "I do believe that spring is on its way at last."